I0739998

Long ago, far away

Long ago, far away

Jeff Solmundson

Nonsuch Press
Winnipeg
MMXIV

Nonsuch Press

Published by Nonsuch Press
Winnipeg, Manitoba, Canada

Cover image by Arthur Rackham (1867-1939). From John Milton's Comus, Image Title: "... the Stars/That nature hung in Heav'n, and fill'd their Lamps/With everlasting oil, to give due light/To the misled and lonely Travailer."

ISBN: 978-0-9937471-4-4

Contents

The Poisoned Lake

I SPIED HER one day in the royal library and took to following her from afar. She was attractive, certainly. In a bookish way, one could say. She held herself at a certain angle. Her own. This land had its troubles but all that was sweet and right met in her slants and skews. It much occupied my time. One day she appeared in my aisle. It would have been different had I expected her. She looked at me, in my eyes. Then smiled and nodded. But by then I had looked away. I couldn't have known she would smile and nod. I looked back, but too slow. Her eyes were elsewhere, her smile gone. We passed by. Well, that was it, I said to myself. That was it.

Not that I wanted to die a horrible death. I just didn't want to live a horrible life. Competition was high for comforts and conveniences of flesh, but I had positive qualities. I deserved interesting enemies. Not to be hemmed in by shin splints and heartburn and conquered by a swollen prostate. Or something like. But even so I had looked away. Maybe it was best. Her being the princess.

The summers stayed pleasant and winters mild. Fields

thrived green. No dragon laid waste. And the princess could be plucked. Briefly, yes. But still. Once a month a man had her. For the night entire. They did all they pleased. All he pleased. Then he was locked in a suit of armour, tied to a stake and burned alive. For the dragon. And so it went for a while. Our city stood. The dragon was sated. Suitors were satisfied. I don't know how the arrangement was arrived at.

My older brother made fun of my princess-wanting. He stood tall. His flesh was chiseled firm. He was a comet in a crowd, affection was his tail. His eyes pierced. He wanted for little it seemed. But one day he said he would have the princess. His friends tried to talk him out of it. He was called names. There were tears. The blistering and burning was described to him by a cook. But he would not be swayed. The armour would fit him perfectly.

That is love, I thought.

My brother left. I could not wish him well. The skin of the princess full-moon flushed, plump mounds of flesh, flat lip-smoothed stomach, limbs supple and stretched, stretched out. I did not sleep.

The sun-kissed morning courtyard sweltered by afternoon. I stood in the jostling throng and my brother was brought out. His eyes wide. He never saw me, did not see anything he seemed to recognize. But I saw in his eyes and I knew. He was a virgin still. He was gagged. Like all the men before. To stop screams. It was unrefined. So kindling crackled and fire slowly consumed him and he could not utter a word. He died a virgin. Only I knew. I left in a fever.

The fever would not come out. The promise of princess-possessing was false. Innocent, untouched youths lured to the fire. My brother clamped in armour and oven-roasted without even benefit of female enfolding.

Rage slithered round my liver, tightened round my lungs squeezing my breath shallow, sank its fangs into my heart. Broken promises. Lies. Pure want not just thwarted, which after all I understood, but outright dismissed. Mocked. My own blood spoiled. No amount of bouquets would move aside the jealousy and relief I placed on my brother's fresh grave. And, yet. Still. I thought of the unparted princess. Between constrictions of rage.

The fever would not come out.

I wanted my turn. I made my intentions known and was told to present myself in one month's time. I did not avoid the royal library but did not see her again. I was her suitor when next we laid eyes on each other. She knew me. Not well, of course. But well enough to nod. That evening we were blessed, the both of us, by a holy man with dirty fingernails, and led to her room. Now just the two of us. A bed. A moon-bathed balcony. A suit of armour.

She was sad. I should have noticed that before. That was my failure. Sending out my want to her with its gaze fixed back on me. A desire not to selflessly explore her, but to make her my proxy for loving myself. As a lover I was common, indiscriminate, rule-tame. She was so sad.

It had not occurred to me till then that she was not the springs or the jaws or anything but the bait. By her father's design, or others, I can not say. Bargaining for more and more time for her land, offering up not her maidenhood but her innocence. Ravished by duty and guilt. I could see all that. But rage had made a home in me.

Wine was brought in. Like I thought it would be. My brother's eyes did not pierce in the end. Suffering squeezed out his dilating pupils like a miserable infant being born. I asked the princess to shut out the moon and while her back was turned I switched the cups on the tray.

We talked a while. It was awkward. But she smiled. We got through the uncomfortable moments. More than many could ask. She told me some of her thoughts. Eyes shiny in candlelight. Lips briefly pursed. Legs apart. Her unexplored sex. I was much distracted. But I proposed a toast.

She frowned, reluctant. It could have been different. That will always be with me. She suggested going to bed without wine. She asked if I had thought about other places. But I was firm. Did she ask men before me the same thing? To us, I said, and we gulped. She was so sad. Then she was asleep.

I put a gag in her mouth and shut her in the armour, then hid under the bed. Later servants came and took her away, surprised a little that I was already girded for the difficult day, apparently. I crept out of the castle.

I did not wish to go but stood in the cloudless courtyard, my face hidden. The princess was brought out. Her eyes wide. Her father did not know her. The preparations were made. The fire crackled and consumed her. I stayed, one of the last. Vomit behind my tongue. It was not quick.

That evening the truth was discovered.

The castle was very quiet.

The next day a hot wind blew from the East. The weather turned. Green fled. Fields baked brown. Dust got in the nose and mouth. Leaves curled like leeches on scalding cobblestones. Berries dried on the stem. There seemed no shade. Then winter came, and even it burned. The cold scorched everything. Few ventured out. Fewer still returned. Then there was no spring. Winter ended, and hot and still days returned. Fires raged through the land.

We heard disturbing reports. Livestock went missing. Hay smoldered. Parts of horses turned up in trees. Then one day she came back. On the back of a dragon. They strafed roads and fields with fire. She brandished a sword which reflected light from the sun or the moon or the fire. Claws gouged earth and flesh, jaws crunched and flames devoured. The dragon laid waste. Only the oldest remembered it. On their advice everything was kept damp. Buckets were dipped in the lake and scarcely stayed still. But still some things burned. Food grew scarce.

I was upset. The situation did not correct itself. People

suffered. I did not think she would be in my thoughts as she was. I could not sleep. Like most I crouched in corners when she passed overhead. But I began to take long walks by the lake. Ill-advised walks. The air was clammy and warm, like it had already passed through the lungs of a massive beast. The sky was clear. No clouds, dragons or dead. I walked out on a dock that had not burned. Fish darted just below the surface, blinks of light. The dock undulated. The moment was peaceful but slipped away, slipped away in all directions like a school of fish. The air grew hot.

I heard a snort. Behind me the dragon crouched on shore, its great leathery wings hunched down. The princess approached. Slightly askew. But so sure of step. She stood before me. There was something in her eyes. Not the pure hatred I expected. She leaned close. Hesitant. Waiting. Desirable but unknowable.

Well? she said.

Where is my brother? I said.

She slid her sword into my belly and it burned. She twisted it, tugging my guts clockwise, and kicked me. A goodbye of sorts. I fell into the lake. The water cooled and soothed me as I sank and the fish swam over me, their scales twinkling. I think I felt a nibble.

There was rain. I knew it would not heal the land, but still it was relief. I listened for several days and nights as the drops thumped the surface far above me. I lay in the mucky bottom and felt dead fish scales settle on my skin. Soon the monster fish of the deep came to me, curious. I prepared for the worst but with the smallest of bites it accepted my presence. I wriggled and reeled and swallowed cold water. After much patient work the fish let me ride on its back. It kept going to the surface. I understood.

When, one evening, the dragon came to quench its thirst during an uncommonly fine sunset, we were there. The fish sprang out of the water and clamped its mouth around the dragon's neck. We all thrashed and splashed in the water, and soon bloody foam lapped at the shores. I was mindful of the princess as she waved her sword, but I had my coat of scales. The dragon grabbed the fish with its claws and beat its wings furiously, but the fish shook it like a small bird. Both their tails swept down buildings. The dragon pulled loose strips of flesh, but the fish's scales cut its claws, deep cuts which flowed with blood like the black yolk of spoiled eggs. Finally the fish, without water to breathe, lessened its grip. The dragon got loose and we dropped into the water. The dragon flew up, roared, spit fire and swooped down, raking the surface with its claws. The fish leapt high out of the water and nipped at its prey. The princess and I urged them on. The dragon tried to boil the lake. The fish bit its tail and tried to drown it. Fire and water churned. The fish rammed the dragon and flopped down on it, trying to push it under. The dragon scratched free. But neither would retreat. Through the cooking flame, with scales hissing, the fish sprang up and again got its mouth around the dragon's throat. The dragon lifted them both out of the water. The fish crunched its neck, bones snapping and popping, while the dragon gutted the fish with its razor claws. Both died, collapsing into the lake, poisoning it with their blood and bile and soon-to-be disintegrating flesh.

In the now murky water the princess and I looked at each other, empty of fury, neither with any wish to fight. I showed her the currents. She tried to wriggle and dart.

No one stayed in the surrounding country. Whatever could not leave wilted or soured. Colours drained. Everything in and around the lake eventually died, leaving just the two of us. We tried to make it work for a while. But now we no longer speak.

French Postcards
New   **Genuine**   **Candid**

Maggie and Jiggs, Lulu and the Baron, Polynesian Pleasure, Boudoir Tableau, Blindfold Bluff, Sweetheart's Strange Request, On the Ottoman, Chorus Girl Love, Caveman Love, Whipping in the Woodshed, The Naughty Neighbor, Sailors on Shore, Through the Keyhole, Behind the Nunnery, Harem Love, Canoe Love, Spicy Acrobat Adventures, French Men and Women in Passionate Love Poses. Complete set, 47 pictures, Intimate, Instructional. Actual photos. Glossy finish. All of above sent for only 12 *fr*. Remit cash, money order or stamps and prompt delivery is assured.

Français Cartes Postales Ltd.
M. Lune Poste Restante, bureaux d'arrondissement, Paris

School for Seduction

A POLICEMAN HAD come round looking for M. Alphonse _________ the previous Tuesday and so he didn't have his pistol when he sat down at a window table in a small café on the rue de Lappe. Spring not quite here and the weather tinged brown, the windows and walls tinted in a tobacco-hued film formed before the current proprietor was born. Alphonse sipped coffee black as tar and silently cursed himself, his luck. A man in the back stared hard at him, intermittently tried hard not to stare. A jealous husband. He was well familiar with the type. Alphonse glanced around, his expression fixed, a little bored, a little amused. The café was full of men able, willing and equipped to do harm. Indeed, there was a surplus of such men in the 11th Arrondissement, in France, in all of Europe, in the years after the war. A little caution was always necessary. His problem in the back was not an imposing man. And he'd handled imposing men. Alphonse began the war with Havas doing his shooting with a camera, but it couldn't last, trenches brimming over with ruined comrades, and by the end he was a real soldier, bullets and bayonets. Reluctant, but capable. And resourceful, of course. Now it was les années folles, and Alphonse, a lifelong Parisienne, had come home to live, to indulge. He would not apologize to God or man for smooth skin in his mouth, for half-removed clothes, for anything.

Alphonse finished his coffee, ordered another. But what if? Perhaps the stranger was here on business. Alphonse derived his modest income from postcards. There were, like any business, competitors. Unhappy parties. He turned his shoulders towards the window, undid a button on his shirt, slid his brown envelope inside. Tugged at his coat, did up the button. He stood, went to the back alley to relieve himself. In passing the stranger he smiled and nodded.

"Good afternoon, M'sieur."

"Good afternoon, M'sieur."

The stranger wore a shapeless cap and a worn coat. But it was – wrong. Something of Passy, the 16th Arrondissement, clung to him like perfume water. Wealth and privilege, it got in the pores, and the accent, it was there too. A man between fortunes, in reduced circumstances? No, thought Alphonse. He stepped out the back and moved along the alley. Disappeared around a corner. Down another alley, across a wide boulevard and to the next street, a side street. Through a hotel lobby, rooms by the hour, out the back. Alphonse considered the metro, decided against it, walked along the sidewalk, head down. He stepped into another alley and – the stranger, his arm raised.

Alphonse fell, dazed. Something in the stranger's hand. Another lighter tap, but still not pleasant. The stranger kicked him in the belly, putting creases in his postcards.

"A misunderstanding, M'sieur."

The stranger pulled at Alphonse's shirt, two buttons came away. He plucked up the envelope. "Oh, Alphonse." He shook his head in mock disapproval. "Should I show these to the Sureté?"

"A letter to my mother."

"You show your mother such things?"

"A gift for you."

"I don't want pictures." He tossed them onto Alphonse's chest. "I want us to be friends. I want us to have an interesting conversation. My name is Erich." He kneeled, extended his hand. Alphonse, expecting to be kicked again, shook it.

"A conversation?"

"Yes."

"What about?"

"I want you to tell me about the School for Seduction."

"I don't know if I can help you," said Alphonse. Back to the rue de Lappe, down a few steps to a bistro already becoming busy, pimps, Apaches, whores, the occasional poet. A private booth, poorly lit, but Erich caught the proprietor's eye, ordered more wine with a mild gesture.

"I know it exists. Don't deny it."

"This school, it would be very discreet, very exclusive."

"I have friends. Money."

"It does not matter." A lie. "How did you come to hear of it?"

"It does not matter."

Alphonse appraised Erich. He was attractive, lively eyes, but had a slight frame, and his features were touched with a certain foppishness. His wealth would ease his way deep into feminine confidences, but still Alphonse could well imagine the man was ofttimes disappointed of a late hour.

"I am a man who can put sugar on your tongue or lemon juice in your eye." Erich smiled. Just friendly talk. He poured the wine. "I imagined we would be confidantes, like schoolmates."

Pleasure abounded, waiting to be had, to be plucked, brought rumbling to the surface by firm and supple flesh.

Pliant under fingers, quivering under tongue, better than a feast.

"What do you want to know?"

"No. You."

Alphonse sighed. He knew nothing of the man, but he knew he came from money. Sometimes it's enough. Most times.

"It has been around a long time. They say the Middle Ages. I doubt that very much, but, I would say a hundred years at least. Its knowledge is sophisticated and extensive, gathered they say from the Near East, the Far East, Africa and other places, who knows where. There are some strange rituals."

Erich strained forward, sipped his wine without looking at it.

"It's survived by staying quiet and small. In Paris, two or three dozen men have been schooled in its arts. Elsewhere, I cannot say. Students are taken infrequently."

"There are instructors?"

"Three or four, that I've met. But graduates help teach as well. Few graduates ever truly leave the school. They return for advanced studies. Students may pass in six months or a year, but some of the techniques take years to master. The theories, the catechisms, the practicum, none of it is easy." Alphonse leaned back, ah the old student days, a teasing pause, let his glass be refilled. "You know of Roderick?"

Erich shook his head.

"A brilliant man. A little mad, but – " Alphonse shrugged. "Came from Russia, years ago. His cousin was Rasputin, you've heard of him? Roderick, unusual talents like that. That family, I can only imagine. Roderick was a spiritualist, a lover of a countess, a pimp, and a world traveler, very necessarily in that order. He was a spy, on the wrong side somewhere, a marriage arranger, and back to St. Petersburg and arrested. He escaped by convincing the soldiers to shoot each other. That Russian at Le Bleu Fenêtre, with the missing leg, he swears Roderick had some of the soldiers slit open their own bellies looking for pieces of gold."

"An interesting man."

"Our headmaster."

Erich stared into Alphonse's eyes. "Tell me how it works."

"A calming and pleasurable touch, a particular word or phrase, the careful crafting of expectations and responses. A battle waged on the subconscious plane."

Erich did not look convinced.

"It's mesmerism and suggestion, together with the manipulation of the senses, particularly of touch and hearing. With practice you master pressure points about the body, sequences of caresses, slight adjustments of the spine, the subtle repetition of certain words. A woman has more keys than a piano, but learn to play and the tune is better than wine. Believe me, I've seen it, done it."

"Mesmerism?"

"And suggestion."

"Pressure points?"

"Among other things." Alphonse smiled. "She feels good. She wants. She responds."

Erich looked into space, back to Alphonse. "And does it never fail?"

"Nearly never."

"Show me."

Alphonse looked round the bistro, a country gentleman surveying his estates. There, large hips, well-rounded bosom suspended in tight fabric. There, slender and lithe, dark hair cut so fashionably short. There, delicate features, eyes startling and blue and hurt. There, a barmaid. Light hair so slightly tousled. Pretty and graceful. Firm flesh under taut skin, a tight checkered skirt. A white blouse over softer, swelling flesh. Her body a morsel, tugged at by sinew, ready to ripple and writhe. A pinch on the cheeks, a few light bites on the lips, and her face would have a cherubic flush.

Erich followed Alphonse's eyes.

"I'll call her Vanessa," said Alphonse.

He rose, walked past the tables to her. Erich watched him stand in her way, smile, say something. He moved closer, touched her elbow, she answered something, smiled. Alphonse gestured as he spoke, now his fingers on the line of her back. He leaned in, whispered in her ear. A minute or two, no more, and she moved away, a nod to the crowded tables, work to do. He let her go, called her back, whispered some more, and took a step back, turned his attention elsewhere.

Alphonse found a spot against the wall, leaned. Erich watched, waited. At last, the barmaid was back before Alphonse. He kept talking, swept hair from her forehead, rested a hand on her hip. A longer conversation.

It was like a play, thought Alphonse. There was a pause in their talk, he sensed she was ready. "My hotel…"

Nothing. Then, a slight nod. Alphonse made his way out. The barmaid spoke to the bartender, looked apologetic, spread her arms palms upraised, and left.

Outside, Alphonse embraced her, kissed her cheek, her ear. Hands clasped, they walked to a nearby hotel. Leaving her by the stairs, Alphonse spoke to the desk clerk, returned, and up they went. Pushing the door closed he kissed her hard, his fingers fluttering over her back, her shoulder. He rubbed the back of her neck, murmured into her ear. Their breaths quickened and they tugged at each other's clothes. He yanked and blindly pushed at her skirt until she could step out of it. His trousers fell to the floor and they tightly embraced. She let out a little moan. A long kiss, then their lips broke apart. He placed her on the bed. She arranged herself most temptingly, fistfuls of garters in his hands…

Afterwards, the lobby. Alphonse glanced around, no one there, stood still for a moment, content, and stepped into the side room. He walked to the front of the only sofa with anyone sitting on it. Erich looked up, folded closed the book in his lap.

"Incredible."

Late fall in the 14th Arrondissement. The trees all were bare and an icy wind sliced through any coats still unbuttoned. An alley, away from the boulevard and all its lamps. Dark, the light failing early now. The alley showing a few lit windows, but mostly shutters and locked doors, shops closed for the day. Two men paced, not wanting the cold to settle in them.

"Winter." Renaldo reared his head in disgust. "Salope."

Alphonse took his hands out of his pockets, blew on them for warmth. Thought, for some reason, of the one-armed man who delivered coal in his neighbourhood. Did his hand, sent out of this world by a German shell, ever still feel cold? Does he pray with one hand? Does he still have both hands in his dreams? Use what God gives you, while you can.

They'd had something to eat at a jazz club, killing time. Waiting. A few glasses of wine. Alphonse looked at Renaldo, who was beginning to sulk at the weather. In Paris most his life, winter always surprised him. Alphonse found him an entertaining companion, most of the time. Committed to his appetites. Unpredictable. Given to excesses in the extreme ever since the siege of Verdun.

"Ah, here." Renaldo's expression brightened.

Erich approached. He and Renaldo embraced, then he and Alphonse.

"So?" said Alphonse.

Erich smiled.

"I knew it!" said Renaldo. "A star pupil, the headmaster himself said it. Soon he'll put us two to shame."

"I'm sure I won't."

Renaldo put his arm around Erich's shoulder, looked at Alphonse. "Ha! It took me two years to graduate. Two years! That's longer than it takes a Buddhist to reach nirvana."

"Well, let's find you a lotus to pollinate then," said Erich.

Renaldo roared with laughter. "A drink! We must drink!"

"Congratulations, Erich."

Erich clasped Alphonse's shoulder. "If not for you. Alphonse. Thank you."

A touching moment, a little embarrassment. So, real friendship began. Alphonse and Erich became co-conspirators, carousers, fishers of flesh. Often found in dim lit places, taking their pleasure together.

"The weather's finally turned," said Erich. No need to acknowledge the moment.

"You'll have no trouble keeping warm," said Renaldo. He took one in each arm and walked them up the alley. "Where to go?"

"Your choice," said Alphonse to Erich.

They walked in silence a few steps before Erich said, "The Cairo."

"Bravo!" Renaldo turned his steps into an exaggerated march, kept it up almost to the door of the club.

Inside, a raucous crowd, an accordion playing, wine spilling. The three settled along a long bar. Renaldo searched, found something.

"A redhead! There. Erich, you must!"

"Time enough for that later."

"Don't disappoint us. My heart can't take disappointment." Renaldo slapped Erich on the back, a slight push forward. "Show us a star pupil! For me!"

"We promise not to judge your technique too harshly," said Alphonse.

Erich considered refusing the challenge, but found the girl in the crowd, crept towards her. Decided on a showy gambit. Approached the girl slowly, took her glass from her, took a sip. Renaldo roared from across the room.

The redhead stared, surprised. Erich leaned in, whispered, put the glass back in her hand.

"If she doesn't wave him away in the next few moments she's a pinned butterfly, a buttered bun," said Renaldo.

Erich nodded, saw them move closer, the snare closing. Erich's lips glistened, his eyes sparkled. His frailty was lost under expansive gestures, wide stance, full laugh. But something about him stayed intense, vulnerable.

Erich passed his fingers over the girl's back, found his touch warmly received. He suppressed a sigh, whispered in her ear instead. He glanced over, saw them being watched by his friends, thought, oh well.

Later, Erich waved to Alphonse and Renaldo as he left, the redhead on his arm. They went to his room in the 11th, staying away from his comfortable quarters in the 16th for very good reason. On the bed they caressed each other and started to remove clothes. Erich's companion was soon exceedingly surprised, but in the end quite satisfied.

Alphonse was thinking about how to get his camera back when he realized the man was following him. From the café to here, coincidence? No. He glanced behind him. The man wore a hat with a brim, pulled down low. A jealous husband. Alphonse cursed himself, his luck. His pistol at his mother's. He slowly walked, turned a corner, quickened his pace. Another turn at the next intersection, then on to a busy boulevard. A pleasant afternoon. Alphonse slid into the thick of the crowd, slouched. He ducked down an alley to the next boulevard, less crowded, walked past the metro, made a few more random turns, risked a look behind him. Satisfied, he rounded a corner into another alley and – Renaldo. A little smile, his hat now pushed back on his head. Sweet Renaldo.

A good beast. Alphonse relaxed.

Renaldo punched him hard in the belly. Out of air, Alphonse collapsed. Renaldo glanced left and right with only casual concern, then dragged Alphonse by the heels along the ground. He stopped at a door, knocked. It opened, and he pulled, with some difficulty, a gasping Alphonse inside.

The room, empty. No table, no chairs, a window blocked out with paper. Alphonse's eyes adjusted to the dimness. He sat on the ground. A man stood before him in some kind of robe. Rich leather shoes, but no socks. A wild mane of dark hair, full unkempt beard with some gray, a large nose, thick eyebrows, eyes like a Greek monk gone mad with loneliness.

"Hello, Roderick."

"Fool!" He whacked Alphonse in the ear with a cane.

"Ow!" Alphonse covered his ear, elbow raised.

Roderick advanced on him, forcing him back. "I have been on mountain tops no white man has heard of, I have crossed deserts of burning sands that could cook you alive, I have been underground in caves built by forgotten kingdoms, and you risk what I have gained? You little gnat! I could make you fish out your testicles and stuff them in your eye sockets!" He nodded to Renaldo.

Renaldo kicked Alphonse. Alphonse sprawled.

"I don't understand."

"We have been breached. We have been compromised," said Roderick.

"What?"

"The School for Seduction has been betrayed. Imperiled. Its secrets have been let out."

"No."

"Yes!"

Renaldo kicked Alphonse again.

"Our powers lie in discretion. In small numbers," said Roderick. "If the world learns of our arts their potency is lost."

His eyes could scratch lines in the walls, thought Alphonse.

Roderick composed himself. Somewhat.

"We have received disturbing reports of late. Too many to dismiss. A barber in Montmarte has debauched another man. A fascist lawyer of some standing. It's a scandal, and the barber won't stop telling everyone. Last week, the son of one of our instructors was seduced by a middle-aged widow. In a grocery. Seduced!"

"Well, after all, Paris – "

"She used the Luxembourg Stratagem! There is no mistake! We have a rash of seductions across the city, and none of these amateurs are known to us. What's worse, far worse, is men are falling prey. Men." His eyes bore into Alphonse. "That's clearly against our charter!"

"There are whores on rue de Lappe seducing their customers. A suffragette seduced a policeman and escaped from custody at the Palais de Justice. And with my own eyes I saw an atheist seduce a nun," said Renaldo. "It's chaos."

"The harm is done. Now we will always have to guard our flanks against ambush," said Roderick. "We were the only hunters. Now you've taught the game to shoot."

"I swear, I haven't told anybody – "

Renaldo interrupted Alphonse with another kick. Roderick leaned over him.

"Erich."

"Erich?"

"Your friend and companion."

"Erich?"

"There's no one else. This all began when he graduated," said Renaldo.

Roderick stared into Alphonse. "We are godlings of pleasure. We have inherited finger exercises from Leonardo da Vinci, psychological ploys from Caligula, words from Freud, and I won't see our knowledge squandered and lost by two rutting, careless fools!"

Roderick pulled out a knife from his robes, the blade

serrated, nasty, a little something from the Proche-Orient. It hung in the air, Alphonse staring at it, silent, waiting. Not the life he dreamed, but not so terrible either.

Roderick passed the knife to Renaldo, put both his hands on Alphonse's head, fingers clamped, pushing hard on him. "Look into my eyes."

"No, please."

"Listen to me. You will take this knife and punish the one who has betrayed us. He does not deserve to enjoy the fruits of what we have taught him."

"Don't."

"You will find him, and you will cut away his manhood. Do you hear me? You will cut off his manhood before his eyes. You will show no mercy."

He slept little, could not find rest. Everywhere he went there seemed to be gratification, couples sneaking off to bed, to storerooms, closets, alleyways, but he wandered without joy. Alphonse did not want to find him, hoped never to see him again, but could not stay away from their favourite haunts, could not refrain from asking for him.

He searched bistros, cafés, clubs, parks. He left messages, castigating himself for it. He thought of times together, little jokes and escapades, and it cut like glass. Regret threatened to overwhelm him, regret for something he hadn't done but felt sure would happen. But Erich was not easy to find. He must have realized there were those who meant him harm.

Alphonse walked back and forth through the city. Found staying in his room preferable, but impossible. The evenings stretched on, and he began to hope he would never hear news of Erich, but then, his usual luck. A waiter had seen him, been given a hotel name for Alphonse. Alphonse went to the hotel, gave his name, was told Erich had recently left.

Alphonse turned to go, relieved, but the desk clerk pressed a slip of paper in his hand with an address on it.

Alphonse waited for evening, slowly advanced his footsteps, found the building. He walked up to the fourth floor, tried the door. Unlocked. He cursed, entered. A respectable apartment. No one home? He glanced through the rooms.

"Alphonse."

He turned, Erich in front of him, smiling.

"No."

"No? Are you not happy to see me?"

Alphonse pulled out the wicked knife, hand trembling, dropped it. He kneeled, put his hand around the blade.

"Alphonse?"

"Erich. You have to leave. Now."

"What's going on?"

"I'm in his power. Roderick sent me."

His eyes wide. "To kill me?"

"To castrate you. Please, get away. Run away."

Instead, smiling again. He took off his cap, rubbed his fingers roughly through his slicked back hair. It fell over his ears, almost to the shoulder. Alphonse stared. The knife tight in his hand. Erich took off his jacket, began unbuttoning his shirt. Alphonse still stared, not understanding. The shirt dropped to the floor, revealing a tightly wrapped linen sheet beneath. Erich unwound it, freeing two plump mounds of flesh, teardrop-shaped, with coral centres. Next hips wriggled, and pants slinked slowly down across them, down to the floor, divulging lush curves. White knickers, tight, barely reaching the contours of the inner thighs, and cut low, left little hidden, revealed there was no manhood certainly, nothing masculine.

"Call me Erika."

The knife dipped. Alphonse felt a great release. The compulsion left him. "Incredible." He shook his head. Erika beckoned with a finger. The knife rattled on the floor, forgotten. He rushed forward, a tight embrace, she covered his mouth with hers. They both pulled at his clothes. He lost himself in her mouth, breathed into her. His shirt, then trousers, the rest. He slid fingers like hooks into her knickers, eased them off trembling thighs. A pinch, she returned it. He rubbed her hips, then upwards, she slid her fingers down his stomach. Such eyes, he thought, and more. A flick of her tongue. He pushed her back on the sofa, her legs bent, raised, and slid his hands along the underside of her thighs until the crooks of his hands nestled behind her knees...

A bright moon, dark fields. The train to Marseilles. A window, moonlight. The world so quiet. The clack of the wheels on the track. Under the seat one suitcase, one rucksack. Outside, everything asleep. A love affair, thought Alphonse. Doomed, of course. But, still. He looked at her, the slight rise and fall of her chest, the line of her neck, her face framed by loose strands of hair. She will leave marks on me, he thought. Sleepy, she shifted, touched the back of his head, rested her head on his shoulder. Watched her shadowy features fly over the darkened landscape.

"I've been thinking. Thinking I may start a new school."

The Snookaboo

HE CREPT FORWARD, dragging himself with his elbows over muck and leaves, under brush and twigs. It was all he wanted right now, and it was before him. He could well imagine the admiring looks when he strode out with it in his hand. He inched forward, fighting the adrenaline, which threatened to jolt him up like popcorn in a pan. Another few minutes to the edge of trees and brush, then a triumphant sprint to the centre of the clearing. Not that he was the fastest sprinter. But surprise was his. He kept his breath shallow, squirmed forward in quick, short bursts. Did not risk wiping the mud from his cheek. Just a little further. It was there for the taking. He kept his head low, unconsciously hoping that hiding his gaze would keep other eyes off him. He would be the hero. He would capture the flag. Now.

"Forget it, David! I can see your fat ass from here!"

Laughter from around the clearing.

David picked himself up, stood there.

"I could see that ass waving in the air a mile away," called James. More laughter.

David didn't hide, didn't run, didn't say anything. He

trudged back through the woods, stealth abandoned, look-ing like a Sunday stroller who's made a wrong turn in the park. His shoulders sagged. He wiped the mud from his cheek with his sleeve.

He passed Sean, crouched down behind a tree.

"Aren't you playing anymore?"

"I don't know." David kept walking, away from the game. When the shouts were faint he sat down with his back to a tree. After some time with his thoughts he scratched at the dirt with a stick. Later one of the counselors pulled on the bell and David headed for the pump outside the cabins to wash his hands for dinner.

Dusk deepened as boys and girls began to gather around the fire pit after the evening meal. David snuck glances at a few of the girls, especially Leanne and her best friend Nancy. He stood with his hands in the pockets of his windbreaker then, without being asked, followed Matt, the counselor for his cabin, to get more firewood.

Matt winked at Julie as they passed. Sixteen years old and women figured out. At the woodpile David filled his arms, a heavy load that threatened to tip him over.

"You all right?" said Matt, amused.

"Uh, huh."

They came back to the fire pit, David straining and stum-bling most the way. He had to drop his wood a moment early, a little short of his intended spot.

"Hey Matt, is our cabin in second place?" said James.

"Sure is."

"Do we get points for panty raids?"

Most the girls smiled, a few rolled their eyes. Matt laughed. "I don't think so."

"How about if we have a tug-of-war tomorrow? We'll

tie a rope around David and we'll win for sure. Nobody's moving that ass."

A couple girls giggled. Including Nancy. Matt smirked. An I-want-to-laugh-but-have-to-seem-disapproving smirk. He shook his head. "James."

"What?"

It wasn't her cabin but Julie cut in. "That's enough of that." An edge to her voice.

"Julie, baby, I've got it. Everybody has five minutes. Fire time in five minutes," he said, "We're telling stories."

"Stories?" asked a girl.

"Ghost stories."

David went to his bunk and changed out of his sweatpants, which he thought made him look bigger, and back into his jeans, his favourite pair, even though they were damp and muddy. Back outside, a chill settled into his legs. The beginnings of a fire crackled and flickered in the pit and the campers pulled old lawn chairs or stumps of wood closer.

The woods became one dark, impenetrable silhouette around them and the deep, dark blue sky gradually turned to black. Without prompting from the counselors conversation was struck up. They told camping stories, talked of weather, hot dogs and well water, and recounted activities of the day; contests nearly won, or nearly lost, funny things that had happened.

David was relieved. He didn't want to hear any scary stories. Not even at home, but especially not out here by a cabin in the woods. He nodded, smiled, hoped the talk would continue its course. But he wasn't surprised when it shifted.

There was a gap in conversation. "Okay," said Matt. "Who wants to hear some ghost stories?"

There was shuffling around the fire, some boys and girls looking around idly, not conveying enthusiasm.

"Come on, who wants to start?" Matt turned on a flashlight and placed it under his chin. "Who's ready?"

"I don't like scary stories," said David.

"Well, it's not food," said James.

Kids laughed. David stared into the fire.

"I know a story. It happened to me a couple summers ago," said Julie. She glanced around at anxious faces in flickering firelight. "Don't worry, it's not crazy scary. Anyways, you know I turned out all right."

Kids smiled. Some settled back, others bent forward. David, part of the outer edge of the circle, moved onto his stomach with his chin propped in his hands. He was a little uneasy, but Leanne was in his line of sight and he felt if he assumed his unfocused facial expression he could study her undetected.

"I was at this camp. Not around here," said Julie. "My parents wanted to send me away. I was gone for the whole summer, not just a week. Anyhow, our camp was by a lake, and the lake had a small island. We weren't allowed to explore it cause it was private property.

"Well, after a few nights we started to hear strange noises coming from the island. During the day there was nothing, but in the evenings after supper it would start. And it was the worst in the middle of the night. It was really strange, like a scream and a whisper at the same time.

"That was bad enough. Then, stuff started disappearing around camp. First, if you left anything out at night it would be guaranteed to be gone. But later tools and stuff would go missing even in the middle of the day. People should have been mad, but instead everyone was just nervous. Then, there were the lights.

"We could see strange lights moving around on the island. Weird little lights, mostly hidden in the trees. Our counselors didn't know what to think, but we could tell they were scared. They told us to stay away from the island, even at noon.

"But me and two friends decided to investigate."

Her audience yelped and trilled.

"It was driving us crazy! We couldn't take it anymore, we had to find out what was going on. We waited till dark, real dark, and snuck into a canoe and slowly paddled out. The strange noises were louder on the water. We had just enough moonlight to see.

"There we were, about three quarters of the way to the island, and we felt the canoe rock. We couldn't figure out why. Now, we're freaking out. Then, without warning, the canoe tips over. We're in the water. I'm panicked. I don't even know where my friends are. I just swim for the island."

David surreptitiously, or so he hoped, moved his palms from his chin over his ears. Pushed his hands hard.

"I'm swimming as fast as I can. I don't care what's there, I just want out of that water. My arms and legs are going wild and I can't be sure but I think I bump into something under the surface. Then again. Something bumps my leg. I'm freaking out. Suddenly, it's like there's a hand. I feel a tug. I feel a tug, tug, tug. Something was pulling my leg – just like I'm pulling yours!"

Silence for a moment, then a snicker, a few snorts. Then a great burst of laughter from all around the fire.

Sean nudged a confused David. "It's okay."

One of James' friends saw them, and whispered in James' ear.

David missed it. He was covering his ears," said one of the boys in a loud voice. A few more laughs. David stared away from Leanne as Sean filled him in on the end of the story.

The group relaxed, became a little less quiet. With some encouragement from the counselors a boy told a story about the hockey rink at his community club, about how in the middle of winter, in the middle of the night, the sound of skates on ice echoed off the rink even though no skater could ever be seen.

Matt was under whelmed. He stood, stoked the fire with

his stick, waited for all attention to settle on him. Someone used to attention.

"Okay, I have a scary story. And you should hear it too, because it's a true story. It's about a creature, a creature that's hunted in this area before. Years ago, but still. There's people, some of your parents even, who won't even step near this place because of it. This creature is called the Snookaboo."

There was a smattering of laughter, laughter the kids felt was expected of them.

Matt's eyes flashed. "Don't laugh! The Snookaboo could cut you open with one rip." He clawed at the air. "Claws like kitchen knives."

"Matt," said Julie.

"Razor teeth! Longer than your hand, about as thick as your thumb. It moves on all fours, most of the time, and it has short bristly hair on its back and scales over its belly. It hunts prey like a tiger, but instead of purring it makes a little clicking noise like a cockroach. Tch tch tch tch! The face is horrible, a twisted mix of animal and human. But the worst part is the eyes. It has eyes like a snake.

"I've seen the Snookaboo. But I'll never tell you when or how. Not for anything. But I can tell you this – it was here in these woods a few years ago. Hunting.

"There was another camp just a few minutes north of here. It's closed now. But it was busy when the Snookaboo came by. Its victims were in the newspapers, but the papers never said exactly how they died. For good reason. It would have caused panic in the whole country. So they just tidied things up and the Snookaboo moved on."

Matt moved around the fire. "It likes it around here, but it's been all over. All over the world, probably. It can climb, it can run, it can swim, it can do about everything but fly.

"But whatever. That's not what you have to know. What's the most important are the rules of the Snookaboo.

He looked around the fire, making eye contact.

"First, it only hunts indoors, only where people sleep. Your bed is the worst place to be. I don't know why, but it doesn't hunt outdoors." He looked around the fire, making eye contact.

"Second, don't move. Not an inch. It can sense movement. It also has super hearing. You rustle your sheets, you shift your legs, you breathe hard, the Snookaboo knows. It can hear you scratch an itch through walls.

"The next thing is, don't pee. Not in your room anyway. Pee attracts it. I've heard of kids so scared they peed in their beds. That just guarantees it's coming for you.

"Last but not least, don't think about it. It knows when you're thinking about it. So don't. That's like calling it. The more you think about it, the more scared you are, the more it wants to eat you."

"Eat you?" said one of the girls.

"That's what it does. Didn't I mention that? It eats people. In the morning there's usually nothing left but a blood-soaked mattress. Some people have stayed still under the covers and lived, listening to the Snookaboo feast. There's a lot of crunching and slurping, then a horrible sound like a body slushie being sucked through a giant straw."

His audience recoiled. Even the kids leaning forward shrank their shoulders back in disgust.

"And that's all you hear. Its victims don't make a sound."

"Why don't people scream when it's eating them?" asked a boy.

"You can't make any noise when you're being eaten by the Snookaboo."

"Why?"

"I don't know why. You just can't." Matt paced around the fire, inside the circle. "So if the Snookaboo is around don't stay inside, no matter how much it feels like you might be safer. Don't move. I mean – Don't. Move. Don't make a sound. Don't pee your pants. And whatever you do, don't think about the Snookaboo."

He sat back down. Julie glared at him. David, all thoughts of Leanne banished from his mind, rubbed his freezing legs and exchanged an apprehensive look with Sean. Julie disappeared and returned with marshmallows. Kids took turns roasting them on whittled sticks as another counselor half-heartedly told a story about a ghostly, but more or less harmless, hitchhiker. The kids' attention wandered. The appetite for frightening stories had entirely waned.

Some of the kids turned the talk to pranks played during camping trips past and present, but the mood had changed. Conversation was sporadic. Someone passed around a harmonica, but no one knew how to play.

Finally, the counselors called it a night and jugs of water were poured over the fire. It hissed and smoked and moments later flashlights clicked on, beams criss-crossing around the campers.

David watched the beams flitting about, briefly considered hanging back and staying outside. But everything was so dark. He went into his cabin, which was now lit.

David pulled down a corner of his covers and changed into his sweats, too preoccupied to be self-conscious of his body. With sinking resignation he realized he had no choice but to go to the bathroom. He glanced around the cabin.

"You have to go to the outhouse?" he asked Sean.

"No."

"What's the matter, David?" said James. Expectant, smirking.

"I need someone with a flashlight."

David and Sean put on their shoes and went out. Neither had a flashlight, and they walked down the path behind the cabins with careful, dragging steps. David listened for strange sounds. Further down the path they almost bumped into Julie and Matt, didn't see them until they were almost close enough to touch.

She had her hand on his chest. He was leaned in towards her cheek.

"Why not?" He turned. Paused. Called out, "Back to bed, boys."

David mumbled something about the bathroom, continued on.

They reached the outhouse and David entered, rushed what he had to do while Sean stood watch outside.

They returned more quickly, their feet still familiar with the path. Julie and Matt had retreated a few steps into the woods. David and Sean passed with their heads down.

"My bunk is comfortable. C'mon," said Matt in a low voice.

"I'm going to my cabin."

Back in the cabin David, Sean and all the rest of the boys finished brushing their teeth and readying for bed. Matt came in and put out all the lights.

The boys said their goodnights, bantered about a few fart jokes, but before long the cabin was silent. Not even a sigh.

David lay in his bunk and tried to judge how far the ceiling was above him. His alertness was slow to fade. He also discerned pressure on his bladder, but knew it was just a trick of his imagination. He managed to ignore it until it went away. By very small degrees David eventually slipped into an uneasy sleep.

Awake. He sensed it. Somehow David knew it was outside in the woods. Nothing stirred inside the cabin. David dared not move. The Snookaboo was roaming the woods where they had played capture the flag. David knew exactly where it was right now, knew without doubt, and that unnerved him. He tried not to think about it. Happy memories couldn't crowd it out of his head. He tried counting. Still the Snookaboo crept closer between numbers.

The Snookaboo rutted through the bush, its head swaying left and right like a reptile's, searching. It was over the exact spot now where David had lied in the bush eyeing the flag. Sniffing. David's body grew more and more uncomfortable with its stiff stillness. The Snookaboo darted across the clearing, delighting in its own movements through pure darkness. David's heart thudded in his chest. He knew it did not sound like the heartbeat of someone fast asleep. He gave up his counting, tried to fill his head with silent humming.

Still the Snookaboo approached. David tried to force his breathing into a slow and regular rhythm. His big toe moved, involuntarily. Terror tightened every muscle in his body.

David realized it had passed the outhouse. He'd seen it? Imagined? Its presence was undeniable. Nearby something weird and malevolent crouched. David strained to hear. Was there a clicking noise?

David lied there, wishing someone would turn the lights on. Wishing he was somewhere else. It was just outside. For long, unquantifiable moments he stewed in his own fear. Waiting. Sweat trickled onto his pillow.

He heard the cabin door softly close. There was no mistaking the sound.

David's fear hit a new high. In his mind he could see the Snookaboo down to the smallest, most terrible detail. It crept to the centre of the cabin. It moved among the bunks, making its clicking noise. David was near tears. If his forced breathing had left him enough air to do it he would have sobbed.

The Snookaboo stopped next to James' bed. It yanked his covers down and set upon him. David thought he heard the still birth of a whimper, but he couldn't be sure. What he did hear made his stomach churn. Tearing and chewing and crunching. Then slurping. David tried hard not to think of James, especially his wide eyes.

The Snookaboo finished its meal but was not sated. David

was out of his mind. His hand was sticking out of his covers! He hadn't moved since he awoke, but regretted it now. How had he let his hand away from his body out into the night air? How could he have been so stupid?

The Snookaboo's oppressive presence moved about. Finally it stopped at Sean's bunk in the corner. It pounced again. Its claws and teeth tore into Sean, the Snookaboo's entire body bent over the bunk. Strips of flesh flew away, only to be gobbled whole before they could hit the floor. When it was done it arched its neck and turned its cold gaze directly at David. David's head was under the covers, but he knew. Trying not to scream, to wet his pants, to jump out of his skin or go insane, he retreated into himself.

The Snookaboo slowly, slowly crawled forward.

Helpless. Staring upward. The cloth of grain of his blanket grew larger and larger, till David thought his body might slip between the threads, threads big as tree trunks, and escape. His body was light as air.

The Snookaboo crept closer.

David floated. Forced himself deeper into the grain. Felt himself slipping into somewhere else. Suddenly he was in cool night air, spinning about, dizzy. Anchorless, he looked below and saw his own body petrified under its blanket. There was something horrible next to it that David wouldn't let himself see. But he felt its attention on him. Terrified, he tried to rejoin his body, to bury his face in the blanket. But his face felt no resistance. He fell forwards, lost, caught in vertigo until gradually shapes began to form before his eyes. Swirling, they arranged themselves into squares of texture. With horror, David realized he was being pursued. From above and behind, an unbearable weight followed, gaining momentum. Chased, he let himself plummet until he noticed a dark circle far below. He angled his descent toward it. Something followed. The dark circle was encased in a dome of glass. It grew larger and larger, or he fell closer and closer to it, until he was aware of nothing else. It was massive. It was an alien thing, but somehow David understood it was his own eye. Wide and unblinking. Looking for a hiding place, David stood on its edge. The pupil, with its iris ridge, was like a volcanic pool. Losing his balance he fell backwards into the deep ink-black pool. Sinking, he felt the surface above being disturbed. He felt his whole body falling, falling, tumbling backwards through darkness. Then nothing. No up or down. No fear, no desire, no thought of any kind. Nothing for an instant or infinity. Then, something. He caught a sliver glimmer in the dark. Just for a fleeting moment. He waited. There, another flash. David swam forward. It glimmered again in the distance, shimmering like a little snake. Or bait. David went after it, thrilling in the chase. It appeared back where he had just been. He darted forward, searching. They circled about, David anticipating, the glimmer disappearing and reappearing. Finally he caught the squiggling little thing in his chest and killed it.

Fear had warped his sense of time but David, lying still in his bunk, knew there was no time. The Snookaboo was right there. David felt something cold and clammy in his outstretched hand. Then a tongue like wet sandpaper licking his fingers.

Matt stirred from his sleep, pulled out of some vague dream, then snapped wide awake. It felt like a full, ice-cold glass of water was poured over his heart. He told himself to relax. Try to get back to sleep before the body knows it's awake. Then he saw.

The Snookaboo over him, its razor teeth dripping gore onto his blanket, its hot charnel-house breath, its front claws slicing his mattress without effort. Its scaly belly. Its eyes. Terror seized him. But his mind still tumbled the last piece of information into place. He saw David astride its back, his arms around its neck, buried in its rough fur.

"But, but, but…" said Matt in a sputtered whisper. He wet his bed.

"I made you up," he finally managed in a breathy whine.

But David couldn't hear him over the soft breathing of the Snookaboo. It sliced Matt open and buried its face in him. The Snookaboo slurped and munched for several minutes then, with David still balanced atop it, it left the cabin and slipped out into the night.

A Frog Went A Courting

A FROG WENT a courting, and if he hadn't taken that notion into his head, or maybe if he'd never seen Miss Mousie on that particular day, nothing would have fell out like it did, and a whole lot of folks would have been happier. And by happier I mean still alive.

Then again, the folks around here, from the Bend down to the Toadstool, aren't much given to speculation. Being practical animals. Let sleeping dogs lie where they're buried, where the chips fell, or what have you, you'll likely hear. But whenever someone gives the story a telling they usually jump in around the Treehouse. Or the bloodshed at the Alleycat, if they want to start with some pep. But usually the Treehouse. That's where Mr. Frog first saw Miss Mousie.

The Treehouse was where all the young forest dwellers gathered. A fine place in its day. The place to see and be seen. Miss Mousie was often there with her friends, the pampered white mice in fine pink bonnets. Proper friends, her mother called them.

You see, Miss Mousie lived on top of the Hill. She had a room of her own with a window, and every night her uncle had fireflies set in bath bubbles put out in the backyard. He was like that with her, hard as it might be to picture. She had the best of everything, and mostly had her own way, and thought that was the way of the world. She loved her mother and her uncle, and wasn't allowed to talk about her father. She had doting servants, loving family, and playmates lined up on Sundays to visit her. And she was lonely on the Hill. That doesn't add up to a lot of sense if you've never spent much time on a hill, but in my experience the bigger the hill the lonelier and more peculiar the folks sitting on it tend to get.

Mr. Frog was just another one of the tadpole boys that summer showing off outside the Treehouse. Mousie and her friends would roll their eyes and whisper to each other.

Well, Mr. Frog saw Miss Mousie and that was that. He took it in his head to court her and there wasn't enough common sense in there to toss the idea out. Mr. Frog was called a lot of things, some good, some bad, but to his bad luck 'proper' was a word that never once came up. The frog wasn't a bad sort, as far as frogs go. He liked to croak late into the night, he liked to stir things up from the bottom, as they say, but he was no more or no less trouble than most any other frog in the forest.

But not any other frog went right up to Miss Mousie bold as brass that lazy afternoon gave her a red dandelion. He asked her to walk with him and she said yes, and the proper white mice gasped at the scandal of it in the way they learned from their mothers.

Mr. Frog found the perfect rock for them to sit, beside the Waterfall, and they talked for hours. Later he took her to that spot under the Footbridge and fed her strawberries, sugar and cream. That's how it started for those two. All hurry and no wait. By the next day you couldn't catch one without the other. The day after that they couldn't even imagine themselves apart. The day after that they were engaged.

"Mousie," said Mr. Frog, "Will you marry me?"

"Oh yes Froggy, I most certainly will!"

Of course they were only happy until Uncle Rat found out. The next time Froggy saw his Mouse she was in tears. And maybe a little frightened.

"Whatever is wrong?" he said.

"I'm sorry, Froggy," said Mousie, "But I can't marry you. My Uncle Rat is so very angry! I've never seen him so angry! He forbids me to see you."

"Well, we'll see about that!"

Froggy made up his mind to speak to Uncle Rat and Mousie could do nothing to change it. She begged him not to, but he found Uncle Rat at the Alleycat House and had her wait out front. The Alleycat was a house of ill repute north of the Hill. Uncle Rat often conducted his business from an upstairs room there. And no business worth doing north of the Hill ever got done without Uncle Rat's consent, and commission too. Miss Kitty, the proprietor, depended on Uncle Rat's good graces, and she ran the most successful cathouse in the forest because she knew how to keep him happy.

Uncle Rat was playing poker with Mr. Porcupine, Mr. Turtle and a few more of his best friends, like he often did, when Mr. Frog barged in and introduced himself, pretty as you please. Miss Kitty tilted back her ears and hissed from her stool, but Uncle Rat never even twitched a whisker as Mr. Frog announced his intentions towards Mousie. That was strange, because nobody ever told Uncle Rat what was what, and he couldn't have been used to it. But Uncle Rat was calm as anything until Mr. Frog finished, and for a good long pause after.

"So. You're the pollywog that wants to marry my niece. You don't look like much to me. Does he look like much to you, Mr. Turtle?"

"He doesn't look like much to me."

"You don't look like much to Mr. Turtle."

Uncle Rat's temper exploded. He punched Mr. Frog in the groin and slammed his head onto the table. The poker chips got all mixed up but no one touched them.

"For this you ruin my game? For this?" He slammed his head onto the table again and again, getting blood on the playing cards. He threw him to the floor and began kicking him. "You stupid woggle! You crazy stupid woggle!"

Uncle Rat's friends looked at each other. They got very uneasy when Uncle Rat got like this.

Mr. Frog rolled over and over with the kicks. He felt his lip split open. The blows made his face feel sandy pin needles, then numb. Finally Uncle Rat stopped. "Now apologize to me pollywog! Apologize to me."

Mr. Frog apologized. All the onlookers hooted and jeered.

"Now tell me you're not good enough for my niece."

Mr. Frog told him he wasn't good enough for his niece.

"Now kiss my paw."

Mr. Frog kissed his paw with his swollen, bloody mouth.

"Get him out of here." Uncle Rat wiped his matted paw clean with Mr. Porcupine's handkerchief.

Mr. Frog was thrown out back. If only they'd thrown him out the front door, where Miss Mousie waited, it might've been all different. But they didn't.

Mr. Frog was hurt bad but he couldn't stand it. He should have gone straight back to Miss Mousie. He should have run away with her, or gone to church with her. Or hide in another part of the woods and never see her again. But he didn't do any of those things, he went home and got his gun.

Mousie was still out front waiting like she'd promised when Froggy let himself in the back door. Froggy walked upstairs and stood right behind Uncle Rat. Not one creature stirred or said a word. Everyone just stared. Uncle Rat didn't look up from his cards, but he said, "That better not be who I think it is."

Mr. Frog put a bullet in the back of his head.

Well, that put quite the bee in everyone's bonnet down at the Alleycat. Animals stampeded back and forth, doors opened and slammed shut, and every piece of furniture was knocked over as animals dived for cover. There were awful screams. Miss Kitty, hissing and caterwauling, jumped on Mr. Frog and tried to claw his eyes out. Mr. Frog pulled her off and threw her over the railing down the stairs. He fired into the floor and ceiling, trying to make his way out. Poor Mr. Turtle accidentally found himself in his path and was shot in the leg. But since no one really tried to stop him, Mr. Frog made it down the stairs and outside.

Mr. Frog and Miss Mousie rushed quick as can be to Mousie's home and began throwing her things in a suitcase. It was a lot for Mousie to take in but her love for Mr. Frog, and seeing his battered face, settled things quick. When Mrs. Mouse saw what was going on she went hysterical. She screamed and pulled her whiskers. "Mouse, stop it, this instant!" But she continued packing. Mrs. Mouse spit at Mr. Frog, "You! You… you pond-trash! Get away from my daughter!" But Mr. Frog just pushed past her. As they ran down the steps they heard her Mother at the door. "Mousie, don't you dare leave this house! You wait till your uncle finds out!"

Then they were gone.

Meanwhile, as they say, Detective Badger and Detective Raccoon arrived at the Alleycat and tried to sort out the mess. They put in a call for a crew of bloodhounds to sniff around. The witnesses were uncooperative, to put it nicely, and it was tough going trying to figure out what happened. Miss Kitty had a broken collarbone, but when they asked her who was responsible she took hold of her tongue and said nothing. Mr. Turtle said it was two strangers and suddenly it was two strangers, everyone agreed.

"What did they look like?" asked Detective Badger.

Tall and thin said some.

"What did they look like?" asked Detective Raccoon.

Short and heavy said others.

Detective Badger and Detective Raccoon looked at each other and sighed. They were expecting more trouble.

That night Froggy and Mousie spent the night in a sheltered garden, from which they could look out and see the Treehouse. It was while dozing off to sleep that Mousie remembered she'd forgotten her favourite stuffed toy.

The next day Froggy and Mousie talked everything over and decided to leave the forest sooner than soon. But they needed money. Froggy told Mousie about the stash he had gathered with his friends Mr. Rabbit and Mr. Squirrel. Mr. Squirrel knew some guys, so the three of them had gathered a stash together and were sitting on it for awhile, maybe until winter, before dumping it for a healthy profit. Right now the stash was hidden under a tree stump where only the three of them knew. They decided to go get the stash and try and sell it somewhere, preferably south of the Hill, where Uncle Rat didn't have so many good friends.

Well they found the stash lickety-split and Mr. Frog decided the Toadstool might be the place to take it first. Mr. Frog wasn't too familiar with the forest south of the Hill, and Miss Mousie had never even been, but he knew about the Toadstool. The Toadstool was a den of iniquity and other such things, one of the biggest dens south of the Hill, and none of Uncle Rat's animals had their paws in it. It was run by Mr. Fox, and Mr. Fox was one of the few who didn't take their orders from Uncle Rat. This was because he was shrewd and clever, and because of his second-in-command, Mr. Mongoose, a vicious, unpredictable enforcer who'd bite you as soon as look at you. In a tough forest, Mr. Mongoose was one of the toughest. And craziest. Froggy wanted to go alone, but Mousie would have none of it. He saw he would have to give in, so he gave her his switchblade and tried his best to warn her about the kind of animals they would be dealing with, without giving her the ugly details.

They entered the Toadstool. It was dank and dark and bitter inside.

"What a strange place this is," said Mousie.

"I know, but this may be our only way out," said Froggy. A big hog stepped in front of them before they reached the bar.

"Just who are you?" he boomed.

"My name is Mr. Frog. I want to sell Mr. Fox something."

The hog snorted. "Wait here." He disappeared in back, came out a moment later and led them to a door in the back. He frisked Mr. Frog and took his gun, grunting not in a surprised way when he found it, but not in what you'd call a friendly way either. He just looked Miss Mousie up and down with his beady eyes and grunted, and this grunt made Mr. Frog and Miss Mousie very uncomfortable indeed. The hog smiled and knocked on the door three times, knockity knock. The door opened. Mr. Fox was sitting behind a desk, his paws folded in his lap. Mr. Mongoose was standing next to the desk. Sitting back on a couch were a hedgehog and another hog. Mr. Frog and Mr. Fox made friends and then got down to business.

"So, what is it you want from me?"

"We're in trouble."

"Yes, I heard," said Mr. Fox, and he grinned. "That plague-infested Uncle Rat has been a burr on my back for years!" He laughed and flexed his paw, showing off sharp, mani-cured claws. "And he gets taken out by the little woggle in love! You have my undying gratitude." He turned to Mousie. "And you, Mousie, are a very pleasant surprise."

"I have a stash I can sell. I mean, a stash you could use," said Mr. Frog.

"Do you now?" Mr. Fox grinned wider, baring his sharp teeth. "Well, aren't you giving me the keys to the henhouse?" He nodded to his men. They grabbed Froggy and Mousie from behind. He nodded again and one of the hogs began punching Froggy in the stomach. The hog that led them in had a firm hold of Mousie as she screamed and begged them to leave him alone. Mr. Mongoose took out his gun and put it down on the table and took off his jacket.

"Sorry, Frog," said Mr. Fox, "I appreciate what you did for me. I can't tell you how happy you've made me. But money is money. And you and the girl are money. You, Mousie, are going back to your Mother safe as safe can be. But you don't come cheap. You little Froggy, they want in pieces."

Mr. Mongoose took out his knife. He licked the blade. If you've heard any Mr. Mongoose stories you know that's not at all a good sign.

"…The …the stash," said Froggy between punches.

"We'll get it anyway," said Mr. Fox.

The hog stopped hitting Mr. Frog. He held him up and the hedgehog grabbed one of Mr. Frog's webbed hands and held it down firmly on the desk. Mr. Mongoose admired the balance and shine of his knife.

"We could have frog soup," he said.

Miss Mousie cried. Mr. Fox continued to grin. Mr. Frog tried to pull away but it was no use. The hog and hedgehog held him tight.

Mr. Mongoose strolled over.

"Come here, little froggy," he said. He grabbed Mr. Frog's wrist and rested the edge of his knife on the webbing between his fingers. Mr. Frog sobbed.

Mr. Mongoose hesitated an instant, looking deep into

Mr. Frog's eyes, then pushed down very hard, cutting right through the webbing and into the desk.

Froggy screamed and flopped, but was held in place. He seemed to be choking. Mousie screamed and struggled, but the hog just held tighter, grabbing her all over and grunting. Mr. Mongoose's nose twitched. He was breathing hard. Mousie stomped and kicked and finally got her arms free. The hog held her tight around the waist and pulled her into him and grunted. But Mousie reached her knife, and the hog didn't see it. She cut his thigh. Startled, he loosened his grip. She swung the knife backwards as hard as she could into his groin. I can tell you that got his attention like nothing else. He shrieked and let her go and doubled over. She grabbed his gun and fired towards Mr. Fox and Mr. Mongoose with her eyes shut tight.

Mr. Fox fell over backwards, still in his chair, with his mouth wide open. The hog without the knife sticking out of his groin dived under the desk. Mr. Mongoose and the hedgehog tugged Mr. Frog back and forth, both trying to use him as a shield.

"Let him go!" said Mr. Mongoose. The hedgehog shook his head. Mr. Mongoose cut the hedgehog right across the face and pulled Mr. Frog in front of him. The hog Mousie stabbed lay on the floor screaming and bleeding and twisting around. Mousie pointed the gun at Mr. Mongoose.

"Drop the gun, you crazy little she-rat, or the frog dies," said Mr. Mongoose in his nastiest voice. The hedgehog knelt down against the wall with his blood-wet paws to his cut face. He moaned but couldn't be heard over the shrieking hog. He pulled out his own gun and shot Mr. Mongoose in the back. Miss Mousie didn't know what to do, but she was too scared to be nice, so she killed that hedgehog dead as a rug and ran to Mr. Frog.

"Oh, Froggy, please be all right!" She cried. She let go of the gun and picked up Mr. Frog. He leaned against her while she took Mr. Mongoose's jacket and wrapped it tight around his hand. "My poor Froggy. They keep hurting you."

She picked up Mr. Mongoose's gun. Mr. Mongoose was dead but Mousie yelled and shot him a good bunch of times anyway, then led Froggy out the door leading to the back lane. No one followed.

It certainly didn't take long for Detective Badger and Detective Raccoon to hear the news. Before long there wasn't a soul from the Zig Zag Creek to the Alleycat who hadn't heard Fox and Mongoose were out of the picturebook, as some folks liked to put it. But although everyone was talking about it, no one was talking about it to the police. Certainly Mr. Turtle had his suspicions, and some of the animals in the Toadstool had to know, but no one was saying.

"Who did all this? Who did this to you?" Badger asked the hog. He was on a stretcher now, and soaked in blood from the waist down. The blade still stuck straight up. Detective Badger cringed and tried very hard not to notice. The hog had stopped screaming for the first time since the police had arrived, but he wasn't listening. "Who gave you this nasty boo-boo?"

"What do you think, Badger?" said Raccoon. "I'm afraid this is starting to look like a pack war."

"If it's a pack war, however did Mr. Fox get caught out like this? He'd know this was coming." Badger looked down at Mr. Fox. He was still in his chair, which had toppled over backwards. His eyes were open, and his mouth wide open. He looked very surprised.

"The Crows, maybe?"

The Crows were a gang no one trusted, just like they still are today. They were forever suspicious, and they jealously guarded all that was theirs, just as they still do. In these days

I'm telling about, the Crows controlled everything along the Zig Zag Creek, and many animals feared they had their appraising eye on the rest of the forest as well. Of course, it turns out that they did, but that's another story.

"The Crows are out of our neighborhood. Let's try rousting some of our own game first," said Badger. Two of the bloodhounds, done sniffing around the body, lifted Mr. Fox up to look underneath him for clues.

Froggy and Mousie knew they had no time to waste. Even more animals would be hunting them, and no place in the forest would be safe for long. They had to get out now. They decided that after the Toadstool they wouldn't be able to sell the stash on their own. They needed a go-between. Mr. Frog called up his dear old friend Mr. Lamb. He and Mr. Lamb had grown up together.

"Hello, Mr. Lamb?"

"Yes?"

"I need to ask you a really big favour."

"Oh dear, oh dear, oh deario! Froggy is that you?"

What Froggy didn't know was that Mr. Lamb already had some uninvited guests. Mr. Rabbit and Mr. Squirrel had found their stash missing, and I'm afraid they didn't take it very well. They weren't the brightest animals to ever fall out of the tree but it wasn't hard to figure out who'd done it. They knew Mr. Frog pretty well, so one of their first visits was to poor Mr. Lamb. They'd laid his limb across a branch and snapped it. They were right there with Mr. Lamb when he got Mr. Frog's call, and he was very frightened. Mr. Frog asked Mr. Lamb if he could find a buyer for him.

"I... I'll do my best. It'll take a couple of days before I'll know." Mr. Squirrel poked him. "Oh! Um, where are staying?"

"Sorry, I can't tell you Lambsey. I'll try you in few days though. Oh, and for heaven's sake, be careful!"

Mr. Rabbit and Mr. Squirrel laughed when Mr. Lamb told them that part.

Mr. Frog and Miss Mousie laid low south of the Hill, never going out during the day. They didn't risk going to a doctor but Mousie got bandages for Mr. Frog's hand. It didn't bleed so much now but still hurt like the dickens when he moved it. They found lodgings in different bushes, never staying in the same one for more than a night. They would pull the leaves in the window shut and keep the place dark, hardly making any sounds. It was from one of these bushes that Mr. Frog called Mr. Lamb a few days later. Mr. Lamb told Mr. Frog that it was all set up with one of the Crows. Mr. Frog didn't like the sound of it since he had always stayed away from the Zig Zag Creek, but he knew he didn't have any choice. At least the Crows didn't answer to Uncle Rat's or Mr. Fox's animals, and maybe they could get them out of the forest. Mr. Lamb gave him the meeting place and told him it could happen right now. Froggy agreed and took the gun and slipped out without waking Mousie. She would only sleep when exhaustion caught up to her, usually at odd times and seldom for very long. She was not used to this kind of life, and it was wearing her down, though she'd never complain. Froggy wept to think that he had done this to her, but soon they would be happy somewhere far away. Happy for ever after.

Mr. Lamb was of course very timid and nervous these days. Between Mr. Rabbit and Mr. Squirrel, and now this business with Mr. Duck. Froggy was in a lot of trouble, and now he'd brought Mr. Lamb right into the middle of it without so much as a by-your-leave or a how-do-you-do? Mr. Duck frightened Mr. Lamb very much indeed and he'd almost talked to Mr. Duck, but the cast on his arm had given him second thoughts, and his nervous condition had made it difficult for him to say anything at all. Mr. Lamb was tired of being pushed around by these rabid animals. He just wanted to be left alone. He knew that this Mr. Duck, whoever he was, was going to mean plenty of trouble.

Mr. Lamb was right. Mr. Duck was plenty of trouble, and he always meant it. He was a hotshot from the forest up the river. He wasn't too well known in these parts, but those that mattered most knew who he was. He knew Miss Kitty from way back, and she made a big fuss over him when he came in to the Alleycat, purring into his ear as best she could with a body cast around her shoulder, and telling everyone stories about him.

There's always been some debate here in the forest as to who first brought Mr. Duck in. It could have been Mr. Turtle. Could have been Mr. Porcupine. Or maybe some of Mr. Fox's friends. Maybe it was all of them together. It could even have been Mrs. Mouse, though that doesn't seem very likely. But what everyone agrees on, and what Mrs. Mouse has made it much healthier to believe, is that it would have been better had the Duck never come to the Hill.

The deal was going down in a shaded, dried up old riverbed. Mr. Frog saw Mr. Lamb first, and strolled up. "Lambsey, how are you today?" He stopped. "What happened to your arm?"

Mr. Rabbit and Mr. Squirrel came out from behind the twisted roots of a dead tree on the edge of the bank with their guns drawn.

"Mr. Lamb?" Mr. Frog was stunned. He looked at his friend but Mr. Lamb wouldn't look at him. He put his hands over his head and groveled on the ground, whimpering apologies.

"Well, well, long time no see Froggy," said Mr. Rabbit. "Drop your gun. Slowly now."

Mr. Frog did.

"What do you think you're doing with our stash?" said Mr. Squirrel. Mr. Frog dropped it at his feet.

"It's mine, too."

"No, no, you're a thief," said Mr. Rabbit.

"Steal from your friends," said Mr. Squirrel.

"Heard you've been having a crazy week," said Mr. Rabbit. "You shot up the Alleycat?" He shook his head and smiled. "What were you thinking? You can't go around doing stuff like that."

"You can't go around doing stuff like that," repeated Mr. Squirrel.

"I'm in love," said Mr. Frog.

They stared. "That's messed up," said Mr. Rabbit.

"One dead woggle," said Mr. Squirrel.

"Sorry, sorry, sorry," muttered Mr. Lamb.

"I get first shot," said Mr. Rabbit.

"Hmmph! I should get first shot. I'm a much better shot than you!"

"I'm shooting him first or I'm shooting you!" Mr. Rabbit was so angry his whiskers quivered and his ears trembled.

"Fine, fine, you take the first shot," said Mr. Squirrel.

Mr. Rabbit took aim.

"Bet you miss."

"What?" said Mr. Rabbit.

"Bet you miss."

"You're such a child sometimes."

"So don't bet."

"I'm not. You're a sick rodent by the way."

"Fine."

Mr. Rabbit began to take aim and stopped. "How much?"

"Two rum sundaes."

"Okay. Two rum sundaes. Don't move, Mr. Frog." Mr.

Rabbit took careful aim and shot at Mr. Frog. The bullet just missed his arm and he threw himself down.

"You flinched! You flinched!" Mr. Rabbit screamed and jumped up and down. Froggy sat up and his gun was in his hand. Suddenly bullets flew back and forth over Mr. Lamb's head. The bullets kicked up the mud in front of Froggy like rocks dropped into a puddle. He was too terrified to take careful aim but after firing a shot past Mr. Rabbit he managed to hit Mr. Squirrel what he thought was three times. The last bullet hit him in the head, and he toppled forward face down into the mud and was still, except for his twitching, fluffy tail. When Mr. Rabbit saw Mr. Squirrel go down he panicked and bolted down the riverbed, shooting over his back without looking as he went. Didn't care for the sudden change in odds, I expect. Froggy stood up and took aim. Slow and proper this time. He fired. He saw Mr. Rabbit stumble at the sound of the shot, but he never slowed down, so he knew he must have missed. Mr. Lamb was still whining to himself. He looked as though he'd actually tried to burrow his head under the thick, dark grey river mud. Froggy took up Mr. Squirrel's gun, so both he and Mousie would have one, took one look at Mr. Lamb, and crawled up the bank without a word.

Mr. Rabbit scrambled up the same bank a fair ways down, though he had a harder time of it than Mr. Frog. You might have thought he was digging for carrots. But he finally clawed his way up, then hopped and skipped and stumbled into a busy clearing, drawing stares from the passersby. Mr. Rabbit didn't get very far though. You see, Mr. Frog hadn't missed him after all. He was quite a sight on the paths, all hurt and bleeding and waving his pistol around. Not what you'd call inconspicuous. Whenever an animal saw him they jumped to the ground or dived into bushes. He was causing such a fuss that when Detectives Badger and Raccoon heard the call they had no trouble following the trail. They found

Mr. Rabbit on a little side path in the Birch district and confronted him the moment there was no one next to him.

"Freeze, Police!" shouted Raccoon.

Mr. Rabbit turned and wrinkled his nose.

"Drop the gun, hop-a-long, and no one gets hurt," said Badger.

But Mr. Rabbit was too jumpy to listen. "Get away from me!" He started shooting. Bystanders panicked and stampeded deeper into the woods. Badger and Raccoon returned fire. Mr. Rabbit ran and darted around a corner.

"Don't let him reload!" shouted Badger as he ran. He was right on Raccoon's tail. Mr. Rabbit ran down a dead-end path. It led to a dried up well that hadn't been used in years.

Detective Raccoon charged right in and knew right away something was wrong with Mr. Rabbit. He hadn't even used the well for cover. He was just lying there. He ran up to Mr. Rabbit and kicked the weapon away. He knelt down and checked for vital signs. Mr. Rabbit was dead.

Detective Badger checked the alley then came up to them. "I thought you missed," he said.

"I did." Raccoon turned him half over with his back paw. "He's been hit in the back."

"Friendly guy like that?"

Soon other police animals arrived and order was restored to the neighborhood. A crew of bloodhounds combed over the scene. Badger and Raccoon answered some questions. "Sounds good and dandy to me," said their boss, Lieutenant Lemming, before going back to his office. Detective Raccoon took a closer look at the victim.

"Hey, Badger. Isn't this guy Mr. Rabbit?"

"Who?"

"Rabbit. You know, the guy who was playing lucky footsie with Mrs. Hamster and her daughter?"

"Oh, yeah. Him. Horny little Rabbit."

"Not anymore."

Mr. Rabbit was strictly small-time. Nuts and berries type stuff. Badger and Raccoon were in a huff. They couldn't figure out what the rabbit had to do with what was going on. Was someone desperate enough to use him? Was he trying to impress somebody, move his way up the food chain, and got himself killed? It wasn't until Mr. Lamb got picked up that they had all the pieces of the puzzle.

Mr. Lamb could barely speak when he was found, right where Mr. Frog left him. He was scared out of his wits, stuttering and bleating, but Badger and Raccoon finally coaxed it out of him. Mr. Frog was looking to deal. Mr. Frog wanted out of the forest. Now. He tried to sell a stash to Mr. Fox but something went wrong and it all went to hell.

"Mr. Frog was in that bother at the Toadstool?" said Detective Badger. He could hardly believe it. Never would he have guessed that the frog, or any frog for that matter, could have tussled with Mr. Fox and Mr. Mongoose and lived to croak about it.

Then Detective Raccoon remembered the forest-wide bulletin reporting Miss Mousie missing. Miss Mousie, who just happened to be the niece of none other than Uncle Rat. The big rat himself, who had jumped his last sinking ship, so to speak, as of recently. A call to Missing Animals confirmed Miss Mousie was still missing. Who had she been seen with recently? Mr. Frog.

It wasn't a pack war after all! It was love.

Badger and Raccoon knew they had to act fast or Mr. Frog would be in the wind, which is police talk for 'He would get away.' They went down all the shady paths shaking things up, giving the dealers and hawkers a hard time.

Then a very unlucky thing for Mr. Frog happened. He took his chances and showed his face in the Beaverdam, one of his old haunts. He'd hoped he could slip in quietly and sell the stash at a bargain without drawing attention to himself, but he saw right away it was a mistake. It was dim inside, but already a few animals were pointing at him. It was too much attention. He walked outside and who should he see but Detective Badger and Detective Raccoon coming inside. They were checking all the places Mr. Frog spent time at. Mousie was watching the door for Froggy but she didn't have time to warn him. Froggy ran, but he didn't have much of a head start and he was soon run down at the bottom of a hill. They had their guns on him.

"You're under arrest!" said Raccoon.

"Don't even ribbet. Down on the floor," said Badger.

"I hope you're not planning on turning into a prince on us," said Raccoon as he took out his cuffs.

Now Mousie saw all this from the top of the hill, and she was dreadfully worried for her Frog. She agonized about not being able to warn him. She was so upset she almost cried, but then she felt the log she was peering over move. She pushed it again and felt it give. She decided it was the only chance. She put her back to it and pushed and pushed until it started to roll. Before Raccoon and Badger could get the cuffs on their suspect they heard a huge crash. The log rolled down towards them.

Mr. Frog hopped out of the way just in time, and it rolled right over Detective Badger without a scratch, but Detective Raccoon was clobbered. He flew backwards head first and landed hard with the log on top of him. Froggy ran up the hill to Mousie and they slipped back into the woods. Badger pushed the log aside and didn't leave his partner's side until he was sure he was okay, and by then they were gone.

The next day Detective Badger stopped at Detective Raccoon's with two cups of coffee. "Not taking the day off?" he said.

"You can't do anything without me."

"Probably true. It's good to see you up, Raccoon."

"Enough feelings," said Raccoon, and they both laughed.

The detectives paid a visit to Miss Kitty.

"Why don't you tell us what happened, Miss Kitty?" said Badger. Miss Kitty was placed in front of a window with a view of the Hill. I say placed because she wasn't doing much moving of her own, with a front leg and her shoulder in a cast. She was settled on a mound of feathers piled up around her so she'd be comfortable. But her condition didn't stop her from being both catty and coy with the detectives. She had her reputation after all, such as it was, to uphold, and she loved playing little games with folks, like everyone in the world was a ball of yarn.

"There's nobody to protect anymore. Nobody you want to protect," said Raccoon.

"Why don't you ever come by just for a visit, Detective Raccoon? Purrrr."

"I'm not your type. I don't have nine lives."

"Too bad." She winked. "I could give you a bath that would make you forget that nasty bump on your head."

Badger smirked and leaned closer. He glanced at his partner, but Raccoon ignored the comment. "Word is you're screaming for Mr. Frog's blood," said Badger.

"Hssss! That filthy little tadpole trash!"

Badger and Raccoon thought she was going to try and stand up. She regained composure.

"I really couldn't be bothered."

"No? But he won't be signing your cast, will he?" said Raccoon, scratching at his bandage.

"Mr. Duck's in town. But you wouldn't know about that?" said Badger.

"No."

"Funny. I thought you two knew each other. Wonder what he's here for? He's got all those hired ducklings with him. What do you suppose he needs all those hired ducklings for?” said Raccoon.

“The forest’s a dangerous place,” said Kitty.

“It is these days.” Detective Raccoon pulled a chair in front of Miss Kitty and sat down. “Hope Mr. Duck doesn’t accidentally shoot any frogs. I’d have to do something about that. And I’d hate to see Mrs. Mouse’s little girl get caught in the crossfire.”

“She knows what she’s doing. The little trollop.”

“Really?” said Raccoon.

“I know one when I see one.” She lifted up a little saucer and sipped her milk, managing to not spill a drop despite her cast. “Her poor uncle would be ashamed.”

“Why can’t everyone leave us alone?” said Miss Mousie.

“Of all the dratted luck! I almost hopped right into the cops’ laps. Mousie, we have to get out of here, and I mean today.”

Mr. Frog wandered the docks on the north shore of the Pond and found an old toad with a piece of driftwood. He was willing to take them across the Pond, maybe even as far as the forest’s edge, and it wouldn’t cost much. He came back and told Miss Mousie about it.

“Mousie, he’ll take us across for a song! He’s just a nice old toad who knows the Pond and likes to keep busy. I don’t know yet how far he’ll take us, but if we can get as far as Crossing Creek I think we’ll be okay. We’ll sell the stash, I don’t care if it’s for peanuts. We’ll practically give it away. We just need enough for the passage and we’ll worry about everything else tomorrow. We won’t have anything but our clothes and our names, and maybe just our clothes, but we’ll go somewhere far away.”

“Let’s do it. But please do be careful Froggy.”

So Mr. Frog went up and down the beaten path, selling

what little he could in petty deals. Miss Mousie would stand watch over him one or two skips away. The animals down here could smell desperation, and by the time it was all sold they had barely enough for the old toad. But they had no trouble. If anyone knew who they were they didn't seem to care, as long as the stash was good. Mr. Frog and Miss Mousie slipped away, covering their tracks.

They huddled together by the piece of driftwood. All they had to do now was wait for the sun to get lower in the sky, when the old toad was finished his supper. They talked about their future.

"I'll build us a house in front of a stream. We'll have lily pads and sun rocks and an underground nest," said Mr. Frog.

"We'll put fireflies out in the backyard at night," said Miss Mousie. But all their talk of homes suddenly made Mousie think of her own home and her mother. She knew she would probably never see her again, and she began to miss her something terrible. So when Miss Mousie went out to get food for the journey she also called home to her mother to say goodbye. Her mother sounded tired and upset, but cried out of joy when she heard her Mousie on the line. Mousie told her she was all right. She was leaving the forest. Mrs. Mouse begged her not to go, and promised everything would be okay.

"It's not okay Mother. You can't fix it. We're in a very big mess, and now we're leaving."

"Where are you?"

"The north end of the Pond. Don't try to stop me. Please understand Mother, I have to go. We'll be gone by dark." She started to cry. "Goodbye."

The line went dead. Mrs. Mouse was beside herself with worry. Wouldn't you know it, Mr. Duck was sitting right there beside her, and her house was full of his ducklings.

"You take care for my Mousie!" she said. "To think of my poor daughter alone, out there…" She sobbed. "You take care for her! She's helpless without me!" She broke down in tears. Mrs. Turtle comforted her. Mr. Turtle limped over and embraced them both.

"You're doing the right thing Mrs. Mouse. Don't worry, we'll bring your daughter back safe," said Mr. Duck. He nodded to his flock. They quickly gathered their things and headed out, led by Mr. Porcupine.

What Mr. Duck and the others didn't know, and probably should have known, was that the police were watching the Hill very closely now. When so many animals left Mrs. Mouse's place in such a hurry and bother a call was placed to Badger and Raccoon. Raccoon answered and frantically waved Badger over while calling out, "Duck, Duck." He hung up. "That's it. They're on the move, the whole flock."

"Where to?"

"Looks like the Pond, north side. It has to be them." They rushed out of the office.

Mr. Frog was terribly, terribly anxious. His chest was tight, and he was starting to feel like he was being squeezed in a giant fist. The old toad had shown up, and was waiting patiently on his driftwood as it bobbed up and down ever so slightly on the water. Miss Mousie had taken everything they had left over from selling the stash to buy some bread and cheese. She was taking a long time, he thought. He kept his gun out of sight so as not to alarm the toad but felt it in his hand through the bandage. He heard the rustle of the reeds on the shore and turned and smiled.

He was about to say, "Thank goodness, what kept you?" when he found himself face to face with some nasty looking ducklings. The ducklings certainly did not have the look of murderous fowls who were expecting an armed Frog with a big smile on his face. They must have assumed he would be further down, where the big rafts are moored. So Mr. Frog had the drop on them. And it was a lucky thing indeed. He started shooting. The two ducklings in front flew backwards, their bodies parting the reeds. Everyone scattered for cover. Silly Mr. Porcupine dived into the water. Mr. Duck managed to run up to a blind in the tall grass and laid down some proper cover fire. He was a cold one. Very professional, they say. Mr. Frog jumped. You probably know by now he was very good at jumping. He landed behind an anthill and kept shooting. The old toad jumped overboard and swam away, letting his driftwood drift slowly away from shore. When Mousie heard the first shots she walked faster and faster, then dropped the food and ran down the path fast as her legs would go. Mr. Frog heard her calling his name from behind him as he reloaded.

"Mousie! Stay back!" he shouted as he fired a few bullets against the blind. He saw Mr. Porcupine and a few ducklings creeping in the shallow water along the grassy shore. Miss Mousie appeared from the woods behind Mr. Frog.

"Froggy!" she called. Afraid for his Mousie, Mr. Frog popped his head over the anthill to try and spot where all the bad guys were. Mr. Duck had him patiently in his sights and squeezed the trigger until Mr. Frog dropped out of sight.

Mousie screamed.

She ran to him. "Froggy!"

"Hold your fire! Hold your fire!" yelled Mr. Duck. He couldn't see Mousie cradling Mr. Frog but he could hear how she wept. He stood up and slowly approached the anthill. His hired ducklings left their cover and followed his lead. Mr. Porcupine pulled himself out of the Pond.

"I hate the blasted water!" He sputtered and shivered.

"Froggy... oh, Froggy..." said Mousie as she held him. He'd been hit in the face at least once, and it was a horrible sight for her to have to see. As Mr. Duck came up to the anthill he could see Froggy's gun lying out of reach. He didn't see the other gun in Miss Mousie's hand until the exact moment that it was too late.

"It's over now, Miss. We're here to take you to your Mother," said Mr. Duck.

Miss Mousie shot him through the heart.

The hired ducklings circled around the anthill shooting their guns until Mousie was a mess. Mrs. Mouse later insisted on seeing her daughter, to know what had been done to her, and it did something to her inside.

Detective Badger and Detective Raccoon knew they were too late when they heard the shots echo across the Pond. If not for the noise they might not have found the spot till morning. The bloodhounds had lost the flock in the woods. Badger and Raccoon came on the scene in time to see four ducklings and Mr. Porcupine standing over Mr. Frog, Miss Mousie, and Mr. Duck.

"Drop your weapons, quacks!" said Raccoon. Mr. Porcupine and the ducklings started shooting, and the detectives returned fire. One of the ducklings went down.

"You're under arrest!" said Badger. The three hired ducklings ran for the woods and Mr. Porcupine ran along the Pond's edge. Badger and Raccoon scurried after the ducklings as fast as they could when they suddenly spun around and fired. Raccoon, who was faster, and ahead of Badger, fell. He caught one in the throat, and that was it for him.

Badger crept up to him as the ducklings turned tail feathers and fled. "No, don't do this Raccoon… dying is for bad guys…" he said, and held tight to Raccoon's paw. But it was too late. Poor Detective Raccoon made a gurgling noise and died.

The ducklings reached the woods and vanished. Detective Badger heard sirens coming from that direction. Then he looked around and saw Mr. Porcupine jogging along the shore, huffing and puffing, and he ran after him. When Mr. Porcupine heard someone behind him he fired over his shoulder. He managed to keep ahead of him until he was cornered by a sharp curve of the shore. He turned to face Detective Badger and Badger shot him with the rest of the bullets in his gun. Mr. Porcupine was an animal exceptionally proud of his quills, and liked to brag when he was very drunk that they made him bullet proof. But the bullets punched through quill and flesh and bone. Mr. Porcupine flew back and landed in the water, where he drifted for several hours, until the bloodhounds pulled him in.

The scene on the Pond's edge that day never left the minds of any of those that saw it, and all the troubles that ended there shook the whole forest. Two of the hired ducklings did manage to get through the police lines alive. They weren't found until three days later, after the most massive Duck Hunt the forest had ever seen. It didn't end there. There were a lot of questions about what happened, and bit by bit the entire story of Mr. Frog and Miss Mousie came out. The two of them were dead and gone but their love was pieced back together with headlines, exclusive interviews and tabloid photos. The animal public feasted on every detail. It was a long time before things quieted down.

Though things finally did settle down, like they had to I guess, and it was business and pleasure as usual in the forest. Mr. Turtle eased into Uncle Rat's place, taking over his interests easy as pie. Except for everything around the Hill itself of course, which was controlled by Mrs. Mouse. She'd never had anything to do with Uncle Rat's business when he was alive, never even knew anything about it, but she took to it quick. Some animals had a problem with her, truth be told, but those animals took on more pressing problems, like not being alive anymore. Mrs. Mouse was never the same after Mousie's death. She became hard and bitter, and she never forgot. Eventually she had the Hill under her thumb like the old rat never did, and not even Mr. Turtle on his nastiest day would dare to cross her. Why, at the peak of her influence even the Crows paid respect, giving her animals, only her animals, access to the Zig Zag Creek. But I don't think she was ever truly happy without her precious mouse, and she never forgave the ducklings. Every few years a duckling would come downstream to the forest, to set up a numbers racket, or maybe do a deal, and as sure as the sun comes up, the morning light would find that duck floating in the Pond, face down.

Miss Kitty never looked back. Her businesses did real well under Mrs. Mouse's benevolent eye. She always did used to say she'd always land on her feet. Detective Badger made it to Lieutenant, and as Lieutenant Badger solved a lot of big cases, probably some you've heard of, like the Three Blind Mice Murders. Or the Tortoise and the Hare Swindle, which nearly bilked half the forest out of their life savings.

Mrs. Mouse had Miss Mousie buried in a flower garden, and marked the grave with a simple pile of stones. She brought in plants from all across the land, and had the best gardeners in the forest to tend to them. Mr. Frog was buried, with very little fuss, in a quiet little clearing overgrown with crabgrass. Years later, Mrs. Mouse had Froggy moved and buried with Mousie. The story of the two young lovers had caught the public fancy, so perhaps she did it to fuel the legend and have her daughter remembered. Perhaps she just had a change of heart. Some folks here in the forest swear it's because she was haunted, by one or the other, until they were laid at rest together. Buy anyone an ale, late at night, at the Sleepy Hollow and they'll swear to having seen the two of them happy as can be, on the other side of the Pond. Though that's a long ways off.

Anyways, all this is the tale that gets a telling whenever a stranger asks about those stones in the middle of the flower garden at the foot of the Hill. Some tell it different. I've heard it told where it's hardly the same at all, but the one I got it from swears he has it down right. I'm telling it straight as I heard it, and now I'm done, as the telling of it is the end of the story.

And those that as know the story, I'm told, lived happily ever after.

Lullaby of the Office Clerk's Apprentice

THE OFFICE CLERK'S apprentice toiled at inconsequential tasks and dreamed of a day when his life would begin in earnest. In the meantime he concerned himself with the drifting flotsam and jetsam of transactions, the by-products of numbers, and the distractions of routine. He sat bent over his desk immersed in esoteric codes and formulas. From morning to night his ego smothered his id under a torrent of hesitations and reservations. His position required strict attention to detail, but still his mind wandered. He aspired to adventures, rich furnishings, a housekeeper, trips to the country. Occasionally, when his biological yearnings stirred, he coveted rather more. But weighed down and walled in by his little chores he was meticulous in the mundane. At work he did whatever was asked or expected. He kept his head down. Erased and scribbled. Erased and scribbled. Stared at his pen. Erased. Scribbled. A clock stared down from the wall ticking away his life in ridiculously small increments.

He had no family, so when the workday was done the office clerk's apprentice silently filed out with the others and returned to his empty room. He would put on his coat and hat and walk home as slowly as his naturally quick steps would let him. His path home took him through the compounded returns district and the government regulations district. He strolled past lawyers, civil servants, businessmen, diplomats, never making eye contact. He passed by cafes, which he longed to stop at to listen and talk with men of ideas, but which he never did. His room was adequate. Walls bare, a bed, a desk, a chair, a window looking out on nothing worth mentioning. The office clerk's apprentice couldn't stand being alone in his room most days, but could never think of another place to go. Sometimes he would wander lanes, sit by fountains, or walk the city ramparts with his hand running along the balustrades. But mostly he would sit on his mattress and listen to the sounds outside his room and imagine what others might be doing.

One morning he woke with an unsettled feeling. He had no idea why. His stomach turned queasy as he went about his morning routine, and though he felt sure the feeling would go away as the day ticked and tocked instead it worsened. At work he was distracted and made many mistakes, for which he was reprimanded. Clouds rolled in and the weather became gloomy. The office clerk's apprentice couldn't help but feel that a strange melancholy pursued him. He wanted to scoff at the idea but found he could not. Without understanding it he realized a malevolent force was now entering his life. Without his intending it a door was closing and a new door opening. He had known premonitions before, but this was different. At last the clock struck and the day ended. The office clerk's apprentice put on his coat. I'm being silly, he told himself. He decided to walk home without delay. There was a light drizzle outside and the clouds rumbled. A dealer in barometers accosted him in the street but he pushed past and pretended not to hear the insults called after him. He walked briskly through the compounded returns district. Suddenly he felt like he was being followed. Though he knew that was ridiculous. He stopped and looked around. No one seemed to take any notice of him. He made a few turns, walked one way and abruptly came back, retraced his steps, and satisfied himself that he was not being followed, but still the feeling stayed with him. He reached his room and locked the door behind him. Feeling very uneasy he paced the room. Four long steps, or five short ones, and back the other way. He looked out the window. He paced some more. After fretting and pacing like this for quite some time he decided to go to bed early. Pulling on his night clothes he hopped under the covers and lay awake in bed in the deepening shadows. Very slowly, night came on. Outside the noises in the street gradually subsided. Tossing and turning the office clerk's apprentice eventually drifted into a fitful sleep.

He had a bad dream. In it he saw his neighbour Constance. She was an exceptional beauty and many a night her shadowy dream form crept into many a bed. The office clerk's apprentice was no exception. He touched himself in his sleep. She smiled and laughed and pirouetted. But she came no closer, to his disappointment, and the office clerk's apprentice came to realize he was not the master of this shimmering scene. There was something wrong. Something lurked. He called out to Constance. His dream heart and his real heart beat furiously, each one pounding in the other's silence. He felt sick. They were being watched. Hunted. He tried to wake up but couldn't. This was not a normal dream. He knew that. Or perhaps it was only a trick of his mind, a vision that insisted it was more important than it was. Constance looked away at something in the distance. Looked back at him. She looked sad.

What's happening? said the office clerk's apprentice.

The police would like to speak with you, she said.

Pardon me? said the office clerk's apprentice.

It's all right. It was just a bad life, she said.

Everything shifted. An unseen creature, some bodiless

monster, rushed out. Constance spread out her arms. It crushed her under a giant rock, bursting her like a sack of blood and flesh. He screamed.

The office clerk's apprentice sat up in bed. Sweating and breathing hard he tried to determine if he'd shouted aloud. Decided he had not. He tried to laugh it off, but that did nothing to the melancholy and anxiety which took hold of his insides.

He must have somehow fallen asleep again for he woke to find he had slept in. He rushed out to work, buried himself in his tasks, from his desk endured the silent, accusing look from his supervisor. He dreaded the end of the day, afraid to go home. He worked late, more than making up for his tardiness, but at last he could put it off no longer. Instead of going straight to his room he wandered his neighbour-hood straining his ears for news of some tragedy. He heard nothing. He sighed, but was not greatly relieved until he saw Constance herself in the street waving and chatting with the neighbours she passed. Forgetting his shyness he went up to her. He needed to speak to her to reassure himself that she was okay. He said hello, she replied. They asked after each other's health then stood in an uncomfortable silence.

I had a bad dream about you. You died. I'm glad to see you are all right, he said. As soon as he said it he cursed himself. Her friends rolled their eyes. He muttered apologies but she smiled and thanked him for his concern, and said she was quite well.

Of course, he said.

My, what a fantasist you are, she said. Her and her friends walked on.

The office clerk's apprentice still stood in the street, relieved, when the old wall gave way on the next block. It toppled over with a great rumble and filled the street with panic. Women shrieked. The office clerk's apprentice ran to where the commotion was. A section of wall had toppled over into the street crushing someone underneath. With revulsion the office clerk's apprentice recognized Constance's arm reaching out from the pile of stones. How many times had he fantasized about that very hand touching him in a most delicate way? Her blood spread out from under the rocks and seeped into the dirt. Her friends shouted at him and blurted out what he'd said about his dream. The office clerk's apprentice merely gaped. The men nearby seized him for the police. By nightfall though it was clear he had not committed murder and he was released. But he did not escape blame or suspicion altogether.

Your dream killed her, said one of the dead girl's friends.

The office clerk's apprentice retreated as best he could from his neighbours' prying eyes. He spent his evenings prone on his bed, avoiding even his window. He was deeply unsettled by Constance's death. He even felt guilty. Foolish but guilty. The whole thing is absurd, he said to himself. He tried to banish his grotesque fears and scrabble back to his old life.

A few nights later he awoke inside another dream. He was at a banquet. He was a servant at the table. The long, long table was piled high with bright coloured meats and cakes. The guests were very wealthy men and women. He stood next to a woman, saw it was one of Constance's friends, and poured her black wine. She demanded more. Rebuked him. Asked for more food and drink to be brought. She began to eat and drink it all as fast as it could be brought out. She stuffed a whole loaf of bread in her mouth and poured wine after it till it ran down her throat and chest. All the guests were appalled, he could feel their revulsion, but excitement rose up within him. He had never seen such appetite in his life, and couldn't take his eyes off her as she stuffed herself with pudding, bread, rolls and cakes and kept stuffing herself full. Then she abruptly stopped, pushed herself up from her chair and keeled over the table dead. The office clerk's apprentice screamed.

He woke with a start. He looked around the room, expecting to see something but what he had no idea. He panted for breath. Tore off his covers and stared at his erection. Dipping his fingers into the glass of water next to his bed he began to rub his face. My imagination is overworked, he said to himself.

He got up early. He stood outside his building unwilling yet to begin his walk. He heard two neighbours come out and looked at them hopefully. He greeted them with more enthusiasm than even he expected and they reluctantly replied. Then he told them exactly what he didn't want to tell them.

I had a dream last night, he said.

The neighbours looked at each other.

The office clerk's apprentice told them his dream, passing over no detail. He knew he should stop but could not keep from prattling on. He felt an irresistible urge to discuss with others how silly dreams are, to disperse them in the light. He chuckled, nodded, and bid them a good day.

Later that evening he heard weeping and discovered the girl he dreamed about had choked to death at dinner on a chicken bone. The office clerk's apprentice shut himself in his room. There were lamentations in the street and to his horror also some shouts of anger. That night there was a loud knock at his door. The office clerk's apprentice refused to answer it and the caller did not knock again.

The next morning the office clerk's apprentice resolved not to dream. Certainly not talk about dreaming. To work and back and nothing else. He went to work at his usual time and did his usual work, sparing not one thought for anything other than his little tasks and transactions. At the end of the day he hurried home, looking at no one until he encountered his landlady as he went up to his room.

The police would like to speak with you, she said.

He stared. Still stared after she had slammed and bolted her door.

The office clerk's apprentice was determined not to dream. He slept little, and poorly. His appearance suffered a little, his attention suffered more. But for a few nights nothing happened. Then one long and quiet night he fell asleep in his chair.

He was in a grand hotel room, more luxurious than any he'd seen. There was music, from somewhere. He walked around, feeling the richness of the drapes, the softness of the bed. He stared to pour himself a drink of brandy but realized the bottle was a woman from his work. He let his hand linger. They began to dance. The room felt warm. The office clerk's apprentice and the woman pushed their bodies tight together. The walls caught fire but he didn't care. He pushed himself into her harder. Flames roared up every wall but the music continued, so they kept dancing. She leaned in towards his ear to share an intimacy.

Your dream killed her, she said.

The office clerk's apprentice pulled back, pushed her away from him. It wasn't a hard push, but she fell, and when she stood up her clothes were on fire. She ran about the room, but everything was on fire and there was nothing or no one to help her. She screamed. The office clerk's apprentice felt himself falling, falling, falling, until he landed chest first against the blanket on his bed.

He did not go out that day. But in the early dusk he ventured a look out his window and saw black smoke in another part of town and he could well imagine what happened. He watched the smoke for hours, occasionally sobbing, and did not care about those people in the street who stared up at him.

His neighbourhood became a place under siege. His neighbours became a conquered people, talking in low voices, casting nervous glances, and scurrying about streets occupied by a hostile force. Women were locked up and hidden away. The office clerk's apprentice lived on his block like a leprous dictator. He was hated and feared. The people, particularly the relatives of those he dreamed of, wished him terrible harm, but no one dared do anything to him. The office clerk's apprentice stopped going to work. He ate little, and slept poorly. He kept odd hours, and only left his room when the walls felt close enough to squeeze the breath from his lungs. He stopped paying his rent, but the landlady never showed herself and it did not seem to matter. The office clerk's apprentice became very unkempt, and developed a twitch in his face.

He tried hard not to dream. The well of his desire was poisoned. He was afraid to touch his own manhood, began to think of it as a terrible weapon. All his hopes and fantasies withered or curdled. To occupy his mind he counted things. He counted the steps of his walks, bricks in walls, windows in buildings, even seconds and minutes in his day. He retreated from every emotion he sensed approach. He buried the sexual itch that came up to torture him at every opportunity.

He tried not to dream but it was futile. He masturbated and a woman died. His willpower would win out for awhile but every few nights, or every few weeks, a dream would come to his bed and wreak havoc on the waking world. The deaths weighed on him heavily. His bed covers were not infrequently damp with both semen and tears. A woman was raped and murdered. A woman was trampled to death by a horse. A woman drowned. All the tragedies were attached to his name. He scratched himself to distract his thoughts. Sometimes he tore at his flesh with his fingers. He lost weight and began to smell. He curled up on his bed and could not even dream of comfort because it would likely lead to murder. In his struggle to banish every lust, every urge, he tried to see no other human being, but it wasn't always possible. On one of his walks he chanced to look up and see the shape of a girl high up in a window. He had a dream about her in which she died. He screamed. Later that day she died. Another evening he saw a young girl across the street hidden in cloaks, veils, and wraps. She ducked down a side street, but lifted her dark cloak to skip over a puddle, and he caught a glimpse of her calf. He caressed that calf in his dreams and hours later she came to a tragic end. He tried not to go out after that. But alone in his room he dreamed of a girl he loved when he was a boy, a girl he hadn't seen since he was ten. He found her obituary the next week.

The guilt nibbled away at the office clerk's apprentice's body and spirit like rats, but then the deaths took their toll on the entire district. The funerals followed one on another. Weeping and whimpering could be heard in doors and alleyways. Tears carved permanent lines down the cheeks of mothers and fathers. Even in their shops and homes the people were afraid to speak, and outside the mark of grief could be seen on every sallow, hollow-cheeked passerby. No children were allowed outside. The girls and women suffered noticeably from the continued lack of sunlight and fresh air. The street outside the office clerk's apprentice's room was no longer full of noise.

In his room the office clerk's apprentice prayed. He tried to meditate. It did little good. He tried to remember the days before the dreams came to him but his life before was vague. And his memory was treacherous, without warning it might toss up naked flesh from some recess of his mind. In desperation he tried to have sexual fantasies about women who were already dead, but knowing they were dead and the dreams were responsible made arousal elusive. The office clerk's apprentice wept. He felt he was being torn apart. He had a tantrum and even in his weakened condition he managed to make a mess of his room. Battered and sore he sat on his floor. Then his idea occurred to him. Such a simple idea, but brilliant. He was so excited he couldn't stay still. He paced the floor so quickly it looked as if he might bounce off the walls. He went for a long walk and even smiled along the way. He passed by his old office and laughed. He stopped by a fountain and vigorously cleaned his hands and face. At home he put on his slippers, robe, and night clothes, and made his bed even though a moment later he crawled into it. He fluffed his pillow, laid his head down, and dreamed. The city was empty. He wandered down sewers, and water-falls, and slides, came to a landing and walked up the white marble steps of a bank. He went through the district and got on a train. He didn't encounter another living soul, nor even the suggestion of one. The buildings outside his window sped by. It stopped with an echoing clank, the doors opened, and he stepped out on the platform. He was on the outskirts of the city. He walked down a wooden stairs and passed over a grassy hill. There was the forest. He reached the trees and could hear the grunting and snorting. Smelling his ripe flesh the wild pigs gathered. The office clerk's apprentice walked into the forest and the wild pigs set upon him and tore him limb from limb. His sleeping self smiled and his dreaming self gurgled and screamed.

Awaking in the mid-morning the office clerk's apprentice stretched and sighed and reached down to his groin. He felt the throbbing. He sat up. Stretched again. He got out of bed and with deliberate care dressed himself with clothes from his drawer that were still neat and clean. He adjusted his collar, pulled up his socks, and retied his shoes. He reached into the bottom of a drawer and pulled out some money which he neatly folded and put in his pocket. He went out, not bothering to lock his door. With great calm in his pres-ence he walked to the café and sat at a pleasant table. He sipped tea at his pleasure, ordered lunch, and ate sparingly. When he was done he paid his bill, left a modest tip, and left the city. He walked into the forest and met a horrible death.

But even though he was dead his dreams didn't stop.

73

Song of No-Body

THE CURTAIN PARTED...

Mr. Punch was a man who moved from day to day and place to place with no joy or fuss. Pricked and pinned upon the points of time and space, all the motion in his life seemed only illusion. Point A to Point B and back again. He did his work, which bored him, then he did his leisure, which bored him only slightly less. Work, Home. Work, Home. That's all he did. Work, sleep, the toilet, the kitchen, the bedroom, the living room. The kitchen, the bedroom, the living room, the closet, the dresser, the window, the corner. Up steps, down steps, up steps, back, forth, back again. He was unhappy with himself. And well he might be. He was short, quite short, and to make it even worse he was a hunchback. Oh, his back curved terribly. And that nose of his. It was the first thing you noticed about him. Then there was his voice. He had a strange high pitched squeak of a voice, every word tortured, irrevocably damaged, in his voice box until it escaped up his throat.

Punch was closed in by his looks, his doubts, and his circumstances. Every time he had a thought or feeling unsettling he bottled it up, bottled it so that eventually he had a huge wine cellar deep inside, with every kind of bouquet sweet or bitter. But mostly bitter. He never complained, or sang. He wanted nothing the same, and did everything the same. He was mired in the trivial. He was cluttered with little nothings. He toiled with meaningless things. That was his lot. He wrestled not with dragons, but with worms. And so his life went.

Judy entered.

"Punch, how is my husband today?"

"The same."

"Oh good." She gave him a peck on the cheek.

"Judy, let's do something different today."

"What are you talking about?"

"Let's be different." He kissed her on the cheek.

"Don't be silly, Punch. We both have things to do. Just a moment." She went downstairs, fetched the baby, and came back up. "Here. I have to go out. Look after the baby till I get back. Goodbye."

Silence. Baby cries.

"No, now don't you cry. Why are you crying? Shhh! Would you like a bottle?"

Silence. Baby cries again.

"No, now don't you cry. Don't cry. Why are you crying? Here. Here's your bottle."

The baby cried even more, and threw the bottle. It bounced off Punch's nose and clattered on the floor.

"Stop crying. I'll sing a lullaby if you stop crying." His high pitched squeak caused the baby to cry even louder. "Stop that! Enough! What do you want?"

The baby screamed and screamed and screamed.

Punch held him up and shouted, "Stop crying!" The baby stopped.

The gloom had begun to darken the shabby apartment. The scent of juniper wafted in the window, mixing with the smell of urine. The sullen neighbors all were quiet. The baby opened its mouth and screamed.

Punch threw the baby out the window.

It presumably caused a great commotion in the street. There were shouts and cries and other noises not usual for that particular street at that particular hour of day. After several minutes footsteps thundered up the stairs in his building, followed by more shouts. Someone yelled for the police. Then footsteps stomped up and down the hallway outside Punch's door. Punch glanced in that direction, mildly interested. He could hear sobs and curses now right outside his door. The voices retreated, and a few minutes later another set of footsteps, heavier this time, approached. A deeper, slower voice could be discerned among the frantic whisperings. Finally there was a knock. No answer. The pause became intolerable... Finally another knock. No answer.

The door was not locked. Very slowly it opened. In the doorway stood a policeman. "Hello?" He peered in, then stepped inside. "Punch?"

Mr. Punch was staring out the window, his expression wooden.

"What in God's name have you done?"

"God? God can suck my big toe."

"You're a horrible man Punch, and it's a horrible end they'll have in store for you. How could you do it?"

"It's a revolt, officer. All the organs have mutinied against the brain."

"You'll hang for this, you lunatic! You're under arrest!" The Constable swung his big stick at Punch, but Punch grabbed at it and pulled it out of his hands.

"Ho, ho! It has some weight to it! The more rules the bigger the stick!"

Fuming angry, the impatient Constable said, "Give it back you misshapen fool!"

"Here!" Punch whacked the constable, and down he

fell like a sack of potatoes. Down with a thud, and up he jumped. Punch whacked the constable, and down he fell like a ripe turnip. Down with a thud, and up he jumped. Punch whacked the constable, and down he fell like a lump of wet clay. Down with a thud, and up he jumped. Punch whacked the constable, and down he fell like a bag of marbles. Down with a thud, and up he jumped. Punch whacked the constable, and down he fell like a side of beef. Down with a thud, and all was still. Punch grunted uncertainly and prodded the corpse with his toe. He clubbed it over the head. Punch threw away the baton and grabbed the Constable under the arms. He hoisted him up as far as he could, bringing himself to his tippy toes. He took a few breaths and tried to lift him up further, lost his balance and came crashing down with the body on top of him. "Help!" he cried, and kicked the body off him. He grabbed it around the waist and brought it to the windowsill. Punch threw the Constable out the window.

Pairs of eyes from every window and every doorstep watched the Constable land in the street. Nothing in the neighborhood stirred. Then the footsteps in the hall returned. And more whispering. Someone hissed for quiet. Punch imagined sets of knuckles hovering in the air a few inches from his door. Then he heard a mob of footsteps retreat down the hall and down the stairs.

Punch gave his head a shake, poured himself a glass of gin and sat down on the sofa. He breathed in the fresh minty air and idly decided he wasn't going to pay his taxes anymore.

He heard a disturbing wail far off in the street below. It seemed to grow more angry the closer and louder it got. Before long it arrived in front of his building. There were thuds on the stairway, then the door to the apartment burst open, and there Judy stood, wild eyed and clutching a broom.

"Malefactor! Vile nosed brute! What have you done? Mad cockerel! Judas! Just tell me why?!" She brought the broom down on his head.

"Ow!"

"Why? Why? Why?" she cracked the broom against his crown.

"Ow! Ow! Ow!" Punch raised his hands over his head and ran about the room. Judy chased him left and right, clockwise and counter- clockwise.

"Ow! Ow! Ow!" she mimicked in his high pitch, "Is that all you can say?"

"Ow!" Punch dived under a table and stood on the side opposite of her. She chased him again, while he leaped over furniture and tossed things in her path. She caught hold of his shirt and began landing vicious blows on Punch's back and neck. He twisted around as he ran and began punching her in the head. They fell down in a flurry of fists and bites and scratches. Punch got loose of her grip and leapt up. She turned over and got to her feet. They stared at each other, their chests heaving for breath.

"My dear, I need a little time and space for myself," said Punch.

Enraged she charged at him. Again they heaved wild blows at each other until their arms tired, and they pulled apart. The apartment was a mess.

"My poor baby," cried Judy. She looked out the window and noticed for the first time the crumpled blue form of the Constable. She looked at Punch. "And who's that?"

Punch shrugged. "No one at present."

She ran at him. Punch picked up the discarded broom and struck her with it. Judy fell down dead.

Punch listened for his neighbors, half expecting to hear the shuffle of many feet. There was nothing. His glass of gin had been knocked over in the brawl. He realized for the first time that he had never cared for this apartment.

Then, because he thought it was beginning to be expected of him, he picked up Judy and threw her out the window. Without a sound Punch ran from the apartment, out the building, down the street, fast as a hunchback could go. Not very fast. No one followed.

Punch ran, his shoulders crashing into walls and archways on either side of him. He ran down alleyways, across lanes, through intersections. He would have laughed if could have spared the breath. I'm free, thought Punch. No home or Hell, no commerce or conscience, no feeling or law or fear or reason can lay a finger on me.

With these thoughts to distract him, and because his hunched back made it possible to look up only with difficulty, eventually Punch ran nose-first into a wall. He bounced off it with full force and landed hard on his belly. He decided to lay there. It was as good a place as any.

He was in an alley where a handful of homeless and witless men killed their hours. The air was heavy with the sour fumes of the cheapest alcohol. One of the men said Punch was dead. Another said he was alive. They argued for some time. Dead! Alive! Dead! Alive! It went on until the larger of the two said 'alive' and ended the matter with an irrefutable punch to the nose.

And Punch, since he was alive, picked himself up off the ground. There was a low cast iron fence facing the other end of the alley, across a quiet street. Punch went over and tried to climb over it with great effort. The two who had argued over his prone body watched wordlessly. At last Punch, grunting and cursing, got himself over it and flopped to the ground, leaving a piece of his pants on the fence.

Punch walked along the fence and after three steps came to a gap, an open entrance. He stared at the men across the street, who looked down. Punch turned away and saw he was in a churchyard enclosed by dogwood shrubs and yew trees. Rusty orange lichens and emerald mosses crept across the weathered, crumbling gravestones. The grass was unkempt with polypody, cock's foot and shepherd's purse. The church on the other side of the clearing was the smallest and most modest one Punch had ever seen, a stone and wood shack, not even a chapel bell. Punch explored. Nothing in the churchyard stirred. Not a squirrel, not a bird, not even a butterfly. Punch rubbed the red bulbous in the centre of this face. At his own movement he thought he heard a sound. He strained his ears to listen to it. Nothing. And then there was a faint rattle. It was a vague sound, but it made Punch think of a horse's harness. It became a little louder, almost like the jangle of chains. It stopped, and all Punch could hear was his own breathing. His imagination ran with him and he thought perhaps he was being haunted by his wife Judy, or even worse, by the Constable. "I suppose now I'll have to murder a ghost," he said aloud to himself. There was a noise, much closer, and it sounded out in a rhythm.

*click clack   click clack   click clack
click clack click*

"Who disturbs this place?" Punch called out, "If you're a bishop or a grave robber I'm sure you have some wine to spare. I've had a devil of a night. Come now! Show yourself!"

*click clack   click clack   click clack
click clack click*

"Perhaps we could share a joke or a riddle or a tragic love story."

*click clack   click clack   click clack
click clack click*

"A fine rhythm. Just fine. It would go with a song and a dance — and some drink."

And then Punch nearly jumped out of his boots as a twirling skeleton popped up from the ground. One moment there was nothing, the very next there was a dancing set of bones. Punch dived behind a tree, took a few short, sharp breaths, and peered out. It seemed to pay Punch no attention. It was a full skeleton untethered with tendons or muscles, unencumbered with flesh or organs, and uncovered with skin. It was all bone-white bone and dark spaces in between. No lack of body however slowed it down, or seemed to spoil its mood. It danced about with abandon. It waltzed with itself, it allemanded, it danced a lively jig, it two- stepped and twirled and stomped its feet. It kicked its leg bones in the air and clacked its heel bones together three feet off the ground. It leapt about from one foot bone to another, and pirouetted in circles like a marionette without any strings. Now and then it would do a mad tap dance, keeping an impossible rhythm too quick to follow. Except it wasn't wearing any shoes to tap with on the soft ground, the tap was the tap of each bone against another.

As he watched gradually Punch lost his fear, as though it was something he could squeeze out of his bladder, and became full of wonder, as though he could gobble that down his gullet.

He abandoned the cover of the tree trunk, fascinated. The skeleton and its unceasing dance did not seem out of place there. Punch stood mesmerized by the click and clack of the bones, so he did not jump or start when it addressed him, maybe, with its song. The churchyard struck up an orchestra; snapping twigs, swaying branches, the hum of worms boring through dead wood and earth, the crackle of dry leaves, the rhythmic vibration of trees flexing their roots. It all complemented the clacking bones and a voice as dry as dust.

> *traded my skin for a bottle of gin*
> *and I don't miss it at all*
> *gave up that skin to be closer to sin*

and I really don't miss it at all

my skin is a drum my eyes sit in rum
you're a body who's after my own
you've left behind that prison the mind
I can feel it in my bones

desire don't need a body that quits
give the thief and lover their due
if you want it (I know you want it)
then you should steal it too

ask the hangman for his room
check St. John's cheeks for stubble
kill the fiddler for his tune
and pay him for his trouble

traded my skin for a bottle of gin
and I don't miss it at all
gave up that skin to be closer to sin
and I really don't miss it at all

It finished its song, there was a rush of air in Punch's ears, and everything stopped. Gone. The dancing skeleton vanished into the ground just as quickly as it had appeared. The churchyard seemed darker, and once again was quiet and still. Punch blinked his eyes and looked around. When it became apparent that nothing else was going to happen he strolled past the little church and out the rusty iron front gate

The first thing he did was drink too much, then he drank some more. He celebrated with absinthe, the strongest he could find. Quite strong. He went from tavern to tavern in a loud shifting haze. His memory followed behind him as best it could, in leaps and starts. Depths and distances ebbed and flowed like rolling waves. Events around him and words spoken to him he was content to leave in their knots and tangles. He opened his throat and poured in more liquor.

Toasts were made, more glasses were raised. Punch watched for awhile the patterns of people and talk and music. He took a sip of his drink and stepped outside. He stumbled away. He had no idea where he was, but he was not afraid, or even mildly concerned. He found himself several paces ahead every time he blinked for an instant. He walked on like that. He leaned against a wall. Then he lost his balance and fell. He didn't have the urge to get up, just lay there looking up at the sky. He may have slept, though he couldn't be sure.

He was disturbed by noise. A physician and his white coated assistants formed a circle around him and looked down. Someone pinched his orbicular proboscis. Someone else felt his wrist. The Doctor shined a light in his eyes that blinded him. All Punch could make out was the shapes of the Doctor and his assistants as they hovered over him.

"Mr. Punch, can you hear me?"

"Can you hear him?"

"Is he dead?"

"Are you dead?"

"Yes," said Mr. Punch

"Patient complains of death."

"What's wrong with you, Mr. Punch?"

"You need to take your medicine."

"You're not above the rules."

"We will make you well."

"We will fix you."

"Where does it hurt?"

"Is there anything you want?'

"Tell us about your mother."

One of the assistants reached into his big white lab coat and pulled out a hose and hand pump. The Doctor motioned impatiently with his arms, and called out, "Give me the stomach pump!"

"Empty his stomach!"

"Put it down his throat."

Punch felt them try to force a tube down his throat. He heard someone say they would get the alcohol out of him. It made him angry. He didn't want the alcohol out of him. He was the one who drank it, why should they get it? He wouldn't let them force the tube down his throat. He got up, grabbed a big stick, and beat them all to death.

"I'll give you medicine," said the Doctor.

"This is medicine for you! And so is that! And that!" Punch whacked the Doctor with the stick until he lay still. He whacked them all with glee. Very soon they all were dead.

Punch dropped his stick and picked up his bottle of absinthe. Brandy and wormwood was just the thing. He did a little dance around the Doctor, and strolled down to the brothel.

He arrived at the house and entered the parlour room. There was music being played, the clink of glasses, and the laughter of the girls. Punch strode into the middle of the room and bowed to the Auntie. Then he moved around the room leering, winking, nodding, pinching bottoms. The girls smiled and laughed as they had been taught. Punch pretended to chase a few of the girls, who shrieked and lightly danced away.

Punch plucked a flower from a flowerpot and presented it to one of the girls.

"I'm Punch."

"I'm Polly."

"You're a pretty, pretty Polly."

"What brings you here, Punch?"

"It's the happiest place in town."

She bent down and whispered in his ear. "Not for me."

"Then give us a kiss and I'll tell you a secret."

Polly maneuvered around his olfactory organ and kissed his lips, which had the touch and taste of onions pickled in gin. Punch pulled her close, kissed her neck and whispered, "There is not a thing in this world that you can't throw out a window." He looked around the room. "But, as we're on the ground floor presently, let us dance."

Punch turned her around under his raised hand, or tried to, as his hunched back forced Polly to almost sit on the floor to accomplish it. Punch took her waist and her hand and set the two of them dancing across the parlour.

Now there was a Ponce who disapproved of Punch. The Ponce was lean and healthy, rose-cheeked, delicately-nosed, smirkingly-smiled. He didn't like how Punch commanded attention and he didn't care for how he danced Polly about the room, getting in everyone's way without the slightest embarrassment or concern. The Ponce didn't understand how such a strange looking hunchbacked man could act the way he did. At last he could contain himself no longer.

"You must be a liar, for your nose to grow so very big."

"I have big everything. I'm no dainty Pulcinella puppet, but a rough and tumble character. And if you lied or laid half as well as me you would be much more popular." Girls laughed, and the Ponce glared as Punch went up to the fiddler and threw coins at him. "Come fiddler, you call that fiddling? Let's have a song that would shake Hell's rafters, if you think you can."

The fiddler attacked his fiddle, and played out a fast and fabulous tune. Punch seized Polly and they waltzed furiously around the room. They leaped and turned about, knocking over plates and cups and trays. Soon the music had other people joining them. Punch spun Polly out of his arms and grabbed another girl. He danced with her awhile, then grabbed another girl. They waltzed and twirled, then he caught and locked arms with another girl.

The song ended and everyone fell down out of breath.

Punch caught Polly in his arms and held her tight, but dropped her to the floor when he spotted plates of sausages laid out on a table. He grabbed at them and wolfed some down.

"My compliments to the mistresses of the house. Delicious! Sausages are one of my favourite things." He swung around links of the thick, meaty sausages, splattering grease along the walls. He waved and wagged them around. He threw stuffed, fatty sausages in the air and caught some of them in his mouth. Punch laughed as links scattered around the place. Finally he smacked his lips and rubbed his belly. Satisfied, he began to sing a ditty which he called 'Sausages and Whores.'

I take brandy in my red wine
I take blood in my meat
I clap to a vine and climb to its beat
sausages and whores
that's the life for me
Oh
those wounded souls in Piccadilly
will think me rather silly
but I enjoy a good billy
club, now and then
and Haymarket is a market I love
Oh
there's nothing quite so large or loud
as a fair Newgate gallows crowd
where the finest criminals are cowed
Yes
In nearby Smithfield they can tell you
the value of his flesh
I once starved to death with black pearls sewn in my
hem
they say Jesus could walk on water
but not on the river Thames

the best crossroads should be taken, then condemned
raise a glass at the Elephant and Castle
this time of year I have plenty of vassals
And we're just down the road from Bethlehem
so nod and wink at that sweet girl
she's so inclined and so endowed
if you ever meet a Hangman
say hello but never bow

"If you ever meet a Hangman, say hello but never bow!" Punch sang out in his shrill voice, ending the song with relish. Polly clapped delightedly. Punch bowed.

The Ponce sneered, "The tune is stolen from a playhouse, I should think."

"You slander my good name? A lawyer, a lawyer, is there a lawyer in the house? I'd wager there's at least a dozen."

"More!" shouted a girl.

"Madams, if I may address the bar?" He went to the bar, poured himself a drink, took a long savouring sip, and turned back to face everyone. "What was I saying?"

"God save us from sausages and songs and your unpleasant face," said the Ponce. "What kind of fool are you, acting like you have no inkling that you are lacking every kind of advantage?"

"I'm the best kind of fool," said Punch.

"You're pathetic! It hurts my eyes to see you pretending to be a king. Look at my jaw, my nose, my shoulders, every part of me. Whatever you covet will always fall into my lap. I've had every girl I've ever wanted."

"Well I feel sorry for your want."

"My want is gorged."

"Your appetites are only as good as your weakest organ. Your desires are the feeble workings of a sane mind."

"I may desire to slap your head."

"Your desire may lack the imagination for it."

"I'm sure I could manage to knock you down and wipe my feet on your ridiculous hat."

"Well, that's a little harsh. If we're going to bring fashion into it let's have a look at you." Punch looked at him closely. "You cut a dashing figure, no doubt." Punch rubbed his chin as he observed him first from one angle, then another. "Nothing wrong. These clothes were made for you. Very chic. And just a little dangerous! My, what a handsome dagger you have! But why keep it tucked away so shyly? A fine blade like that should be displayed more prominently. Let's try it here!" Punch took the knife from its belt loop and drove it into the Ponce's thigh. He took a step back as the Ponce screamed and clutched his leg. "No, that doesn't look quite right. It would be better in the side. Oh! Very sharp!" He stuck the knife in his side. The Ponce bled on silk cushions and the richly carpeted floor. Blood collected and seeped into woven scenes of mythical battlefields and fabled coronations. "I know just the thing. We'll leave the knife here in your chest. There! Much better. I can see it being the latest vogue. Soon every princely playboy in the West End will be sporting a dagger in their chest."

The Ponce lay in the middle of the carpet with his knife in the middle of his chest. No one made a sound. Punch bowed to the Auntie. "Thank you for your hospitality and a lovely evening. It's time now for me to take my leave. Good night all!" Punch headed for the door.

Polly ran up and grabbed his arm. "Take me with you, out of this place. We'll go away together."

"My dear, didn't you listen? You don't need me, all you need is a window." He grabbed a cane from the rack by the door, tested its weight in his hand, and handed it to her. "And a big stick."

Punch left. Outside, he closed his eyes as he walked, and soon he drifted off. In his tired state he wasn't sure if he was dreaming or walking. He came through dark lanes and found himself back at the churchyard. He passed the bushes and fence and entered by the front gate this time, like an invited guest. He sat against a gravestone and rested. The wind rustled. Punch was feeling the effects of the absinthe, or was dreaming he was feeling the effects of the absinthe. His head felt heavy. He stretched out his poor, thin legs, feeling passably comfortable.

"I could have a restful dream here," he thought.

"If I'm not already," he corrected himself.

Looking to his side he saw a fresh pile of dirt next to an empty grave. By the grave the strange skeleton appeared, doing its dance. With its dry voice it sang its song.

traded my skin for a bottle of gin
casket of wine and a wedding barrow
let out all the air and let the dirt in
it's a hollow man who won't suck the marrow

my skin is a drum my eyes sit in rum
you're a body who's after my own
you've left behind that prison the mind
I can feel it in my bones

so forget your body and learn the dance
the dance where your heart has no home
your body belonged to a bodily trance
now dance the dance of the bones

traded my skin for a bottle of gin
and I don't miss it at all
gave up that skin to be closer to sin
and I really don't miss it at all

It disappeared just like the last time, dropping out of sight like a condemned man through a trap door. The place seemed darker again, or the dream seemed darker again. It was quiet. Punch looked around, feeling slightly curious and confused. He slowly inched over to the grave and peered in. Empty. He looked about for any other holes. There were none. Very gingerly Punch stepped out of the churchyard, as though the ground might give.

Punch decided to have something to eat. He found a street stall with a table and stools and sat down to some sausages, oysters, and herring. Unluckily for Punch though he was noticed. A policeman at another stall had spotted him, and soon there were constables at both ends of the street.

The police slowly and carefully surrounded him. One by one the people at Punch's table noticed the activity and quietly picked up their food and left. The food seller disappeared under his stall. Punch noticed nothing. The policemen closed in. One came up behind Punch, stood still for a moment watching him gulp his food, then leapt at him. Punch sprang out of the way, and the policeman knocked himself out on the table. The rest charged at him. Sausages and oysters went flying through the air. Punch ran around the table. The policemen chased him round and round in circles. Punch ran in circles so fast he caught up to the policeman in front of him.

"Get out of the way!" he shouted, and knocked him down with a whack. The constables looked behind them, stopped running, and started to chase in circles the other way. The policeman who was right behind Punch stood where he was, confused. Punch trampled over him, followed by all the other policemen.

At last one of them caught hold of Punch. They wrestled him to the ground. In the confusion some of the policemen twisted their fellow officers' arms and feet. Punch tried to slither out of the pile but he was held tight. Someone put handcuffs on him.

"You're a prisoner, Punch." And they told the truth, because he was captured. Punch was lifted off his feet and carried to a damp and dirty cell deep in the bowels of the Gaol. His crimes were a sensation, and he was an infamous figure there. There were all sorts of requests to see him.

Punch sat in his cell, awaiting the next morning's trial and sentence. There was a table with chocolates and sweets. A Phrenologist and a Freudian fussed around him, measuring and analyzing his face, and especially his great snoot. A Lawyer sat and tried to talk with Punch while they took a cast of his head and face. Punch couldn't talk much, so the Lawyer discussed the evidence. When the cast was done he brushed aside rulers, calipers, and diagrams of ids and bumps, and placed down some legal papers.

"You surely are in a mess, pickle, and jam."

"Do you have any jam?"

"I can tell you a hangman's noose doesn't tickle."

"Pickles? Did you say you have pickles?"

"You'd better listen to me, Punch. I'm the only one who get can you out of this place."

Punch popped chocolates into his mouth. The Freudian and Phrenologist examined Punch's cast, discussing excitedly the significance of his snout.

"You have a trial in the morning. You could hang!" said the Lawyer.

"Hang science and laws! Instruments that don't play music and books that don't tell stories. Get out! All of you get out!" Punch chased them out of his cell. The Freudian and Phrenologist grabbed frantically at all their things and stayed out of his reach. The guards quickly came down the hall and let everyone out, leaving Punch to himself.

The next day Punch was taken before a Judge, who convicted him and condemned him to the gallows. He was taken back to the Gaol to a different cell, one overlooking the prison yard, where he could see the gallows from which he was to hang that afternoon. The Hangman had a busy day preparing all the prisoners. He visited everyone, guessed their weight, and measured out his ropes. He inspected the gallows, and looked over the caskets.

The afternoon came soon enough for everyone and all the condemned were brought out into the yard. The Hangman looked solemn but joked with the guards. He went to each prisoner and tied their arms behind their back.

The prisoners were all readied. The Hangman looked them over one last time, like a fishmonger with his day's catch. He stopped at Punch, who did not avoid his stare. He wondered for a moment what length rope would best go with a hunchback of his size.

"You're going to hang now, Punch," he said, to pass the awkward silence.

"Why?"

"Why? You're as guilty as sin!"

"Guilt is a poor reason for hanging."

Disgusted, the Hangman yanked him by his arm up the gallows steps. He decided to make Punch the first. Other criminals were lined up on the gallows beside Punch. Some cried, some prayed, some had to be held upright. They all sweated profusely and were pale. Punch looked around him calmly, smiling. He seemed to have his arms behind his back voluntarily, as though taking a stroll through the park. The Hangman was infuriated. He hit him in the back with his elbow and said, "You may ask for forgiveness now." Punch scoffed and smirked. The Hangman could not contain himself, "Take that smile off your face! Do you imagine yourself to be different? You are not! Take it from me, I've hanged more men than you've ever even met. I'm Jack Ketch, I'm the goose of the gallows! Believe me, the rope will hold your neck tighter than a lover, and gravity will pull at your feet like vicious children."

"Well you know your business. I've never been hanged before, and I depend entirely on your experience."

The Hangman pointed to a spot in front of the dangling noose. "Stand right there."

Punch took his spot and asked helpfully, "Here?"

"Yes there." He gave the gallows a final inspection. "Now put your head in that noose."

"Right!" Punch thrust his head to one side of the noose.

"No, no," said the Hangman, "Inside the noose."

"Like this?" Punch thrust his head to the other side of the noose.

"No, no," said the Hangman. "In the middle!"

"What?" Punch put his head back to the other side of the noose again, clearly confused.

"The middle, the middle!"

Punch struggled with it unsuccessfully, set the noose swaying, and thrust his head at it several times, always missing. He looked at the Hangman almost accusingly. "I think it's too small." The Hangman's professional pride was stung.

"No, no, no! You're doing it wrong!" He grabbed and steadied the noose. "There, right in there," he said exasperated.

Punch, with a look of concentration on his face, thrust his head at it once more and missed. "Damn!"

"No, look," said the Hangman, "it's very simple, see. The head goes in like this." He showed Punch how to do it, putting his own head in the noose. "See?"

With a smile Punch gave him a vicious kick in the backside of his derriere that sent him flying off the gallows with the rope around his neck. The rope cracked like a whip and the Hangman jerked and twisted.

"What a fine demonstration. Well done! I feel short of breath just watching. I can't imagine anyone doing a better job of hanging than you." Punch clapped his hands. "You're a maestro at both ends of the rope." The body became still, gently rotating back and forth on its rope. "It was a lovely dance." Punch slipped the rope off his wrists, bowed to his fellow criminals, and went down the gallows steps. He climbed a stack of empty coffins laid against the wall, heaved himself over the ledge, and disappeared from sight. The confused criminals left behind fidgeted uncomfortably.

"What was he in for?"

"Who's going to hang us now?"

"Shut up!"

Punch ran from the Gaol and soon lost himself in the chaos of the neighborhood, wandering the lanes and alleys without a care in the world. He listened to the calls of the street vendors, and watched the pickpockets ply their trade. He winked and leered at the whores, and joked with the drunks and the drug addicts. He sat on a fence and watched a good tavern brawl, and later in a courtyard laughed with everyone else when an Indian snake charmer got bit by his own snake. He even managed to steal some piss-poor wine.

As night came on Punch started humming to himself. He began to compose a drinking song in his head. It occupied him completely, and when he was finally happy with it he began to sing it out loud.

> *gin vodka whisky rum*
> *blood of grape and piss of plum*
> *dairy dilly daiquiri dock*
> *sangria soapstone sips of scotch*
> *lager breakfast brewing brunch*
> *hearty snacks and a stout lunch*
> *portly vessels with which to court*
> *and a strong sweet girl in every port*
> *Caesars cupids and vermouth*
> *causeways cafes kissing booths*
> *champagne moonshine Spanish fly*
> *white cells red cells plasma rye*
> *black sheep clean sheets give a dog a bone*
> *amaretto bourbon ice cream cones*
> *sacred ferment and distilled curse*

come from God and so does thirst
draft nectar cider and ale
I could swallow the ocean
that swallowed the whale

The singing made him thirsty, and soon his bottle was empty. Dropping the bottle he walked a little farther and found himself alongside of the churchyard. He was not surprised. "It's beginning to look like home," he said to himself. He entered the churchyard, yawned and stretched, and walked around to the back of the little church. He came back with a rope and dropped it at his feet. He turned his head about, stretching his neck, sighed, and got to work. He tied a noose in one end, tying the other end to a tree. He threw the noose into the branches of the tree, and climbed into the branches after it, spending a great deal of effort to do so. Once in the branches he put the noose around his neck and climbed out onto a large branch, testing it gingerly with his full weight. He decided to rest a few moments to catch his breath. Then he slipped his rump off the branch. The rope snapped tight and Punch dangled from the tree.

He was hanging there for some time before he was noticed. His friends Joey the Clown, Pug the Monkey, Polly and a Priest entered the churchyard and tried to take him down. Punch would have none of it. He pushed them away with his feet. They tried to push him into the sky by his limp legs. It was a ridiculous sight. They pulled his feet in different directions while he kicked them in the head. Polly tried to hook her bloody cane around Punch's ankles to yank him down, but his feet were too fast. She tried to reason with him as she attempted to brace his foot with her head. The Priest threatened Heaven and cajoled Hell between lunges. Pug the Monkey and Joey the Clown shouted directions at each other as they went in circles wrestling with Punch's legs. Punch told them all to leave him alone. He kept whacking them with his feet, and otherwise not cooperating. They tried to talk him out of it, and tried to shake him out of the tree. Joey the Clown and Pug the Monkey kicked at the tree. They argued with each other, and with everyone else. The two of them pretended to leave, calling goodbyes, then lunged at him. Punch pulled his feet out of the way.

"Come down from there!"

"Bugger off!" Punch landed a kick on Joey, and he fell.

Finally, seeing they could do no good, nor change his mind, they left him alone. Joey the Clown and Pug the Monkey, tired from the effort, went off in search of happier pursuits. Polly wiped away a few tears and left. The Priest, torn between damning Punch and saying a prayer for him, did a little bit of both. They each filed out of the churchyard. Punch remained hanging. Nothing else came to disturb him, so he was left to his hanging without distraction. The yard was quiet and still. He dangled from the tree, unthinking. Days and nights passed, and the only visitor was a gentle and infrequent breeze. The sun stayed behind cloud and trees. The only sound to be heard was the soft rattle of bones somewhere in the distance. For over a week Punch dangled there.

Then an awful smell entered the yard. There was an unnatural charge in the air that even the plants could sense. It became hot, as if a furnace just had its doors thrown open. There was an awful screech as the rusty gate opened and who should appear but the Devil himself!

He was tall, with eyes like candle flames. His features were twisted with malice, and he had horns sharp as knives on the crown of his head. He had a handsome red cloak around him and carried a wicked looking pitchfork in his hand. The smell of brimstone filled the air. When he laid those eyes on Punch his ugly grin stretched itself wider.

"Oh, ho, what's this? What an ugly ornament has been placed on this tree. Perhaps its skeleton will make a fine wind chime." He looked Punch over with obvious contempt and twigged the rope. "Such a crooked little piece of bacon, what do you say to a roasting fire?"

"Your horns make you to be a cuckold or a devil. Either way, you're disturbing a perfectly peaceful hanging."

"I'm the Devil, Punch, and it's time to pay for your sins."

"It's a buyer's market these days, a good time to pay for them. But I'm afraid your offer is not one that interests me."

"It's your sins that have gathered interest, and you pay for them whether you want to or not," snorted the Devil.

"You have a reputation as a terrible Landlord."

"Terrible and a thousand times terrible!" he roared. "That's the point! You're one of the damned, and you'll soon be feeling many points." He held the prongs of his pitchfork one hair's breadth beneath Punch's ample nose.

"It does not sound very promising."

The Devil bent down to be level with Punch's head. "I'm going to drag you off to Hell."

"Let's have some music. If they're unburdened from guilt, sins can really carry a tune. Let me risk immodesty, I've fiddled with my virtue, and found it wanting," said Punch. The Devil ignored him, and began to lift him up. Punch tweaked his nose.

"Enough!" the Devil shouted, very angry. With one blow he knocked Punch out of the rope and tree. "Addlebrained, insolent little man. Do you imagine that offensive nose of yours gives you the right to thumb your nose at me? It is not so. I'll use your crooked backbone to pick my teeth." He reached out for Punch with a large brutish hand.

"I admire the glint of your eye, the thrust of your pitchfork. You're not without a certain rebellious charm, but you serve your purpose as given to you. I myself don't serve any purpose."

The Devil turned red as a hot coal, brimming with pure rage. "Hambone! Penny gaffer! Amateur! I'm the greatest mutineer there ever was! You're nothing but an earthly vandal."

"That's the way to do it!" said Punch as he picked up a big stick and whacked the Devil over the head. Shocked and outraged the Devil whacked Punch with his pitchfork. They stared at each other a moment, feeling the pain in their heads, then both erupted into a storm of swings and blows.

Punch hit the Devil straight down on the top of his head, then the Devil did the same. They went back and forth, and in little circles, landing vicious blows. The butt end of the Devil's pitchfork caught Punch's nose, and it stung smartly. Punch rained down blows on the Devil's head until one of his horns was slightly bent.

"Doomed little hunchback!" yelled the Devil.

"Feeling tired yet, Old Nick?" said Punch.

They renewed their assaults, circling each other, jabbing and swinging. They walloped and thwacked and kicked each other. Their blows were wild and furious. They broke apart and panted for breath.

"You may know how to dance, but your pitchfork is beginning to sag," said Punch.

"Your face will be useful for scrubbing the calluses off my feet," replied the Devil, amoung more wallops and whacks. They both continued to take a licking.

"Go find yourself another soul for your cupboard, you old woman."

"The first thing I shall do in Hell is take out your vocal cords," said the Devil. "You must be a eunuch for your voice to be so high and squeaky."

"My voice? Have you heard your voice? So soft and puny it is that I hardly understand you."

The Devil drew himself up. "My voice can make mountains shake like rice pudding."

"What's that? I can't hear you," said Punch, leaning forward.

The Devil opened wide his mouth and roared. The wind turned hot, the foul smell of his breath rushed over the meadow, and all other noises were drowned out. Flowers wilted before it.

"Did you say something, Old Nick?"

The Devil opened his mouth wider and roared again. It was near deafening. The air screeched, birds belched dumb silence.

"There's plenty of dead here, but I don't see them waking," said Punch, looking around.

The Devil roared again, opening his mouth even wider. This time Punch grabbed his jaws, forced them open wider still, and dived in. He crawled into his mouth and down his throat. The Devil, eyes wide open in surprise, thrashed about the churchyard. He held his belly and looked very sick. He groaned and stumbled against trees and gravestones. Punch knocked the Devil's organs about. He squeezed his liver, he punched his lungs, he elbowed his pancreas, he kneed his kidney and he bit his spleen. He kicked his stomach from the inside until it burst open and out he popped. The Devil was dead.

Punch laughed, and did a lively little dance around him. And, since he was still alive, he left the churchyard, never to return. But also, never to go back. So off he went. Out somewhere.

And that's where he is today.

Far Away

THE MAN TRIED to kiss her but her mouth moved. He touched her, but she dropped out of reach. He tried to hold her hands, but they wouldn't stay still. He tried to feel her skin but the clothes were in the way. He tried to look in her eyes, but they were looking far away. He sat on her bed, but she laid on the living room couch. He touched the back of her neck, but it turned and went away. He followed, but she would not lead.

They met again in the next life, and he decided to do it right this time. She was a clever girl, and she read the book on Italian Politics.

"I'm going to marry the King of Tunisia," she said.

So to be near her he pretended he was blind. He rescued a dog from the circus to be his seeing eye dog. The dog was blind, but it could ride a unicycle, and he taught it how to tune a piano.

Every day he passed by her clay and brick mansion, pretending to be a blind man, led by his blind seeing eye dog. Usually the woman looked out to sea. Sometimes though she watched the people in the street. One time she came down and fed the dog lobster and duck. The man licked his lips. He explained to her how the first gods used to eat their own children because they loved them too much. Then he told her that she was beautiful enough to eat.

"But you're blind," she said.

"My little dog told me," he said.

But she ran off with a sea captain. He took her to the West Indies one night in the middle of a storm. The man picked up the dog and went for a walk.

The dog led them to the island of Guadeloupe, where they bought a bar on the beach. They searched for the perfect margarita, believing that might cause fate to bring her back to them. But fate was in a prison in Argentina, and not in a clever mood.

The man took a real estate course and moved to Montana. The dog came along when he heard they had a good Mexican restaurant. It was quiet out there, and they watched a lot of TV. Actually though only the man watched it, since the dog was blind. The man watched and described what was happening to the dog.

The woman read love poems from an Argentinean cowboy. They lived in the hills together. Then one day he announced he must follow his dream, that the two of them were going to the Yukon, and she left him.

"You can take a girl to sea, but you can't take a girl to see the ocean," she said.

The man found her in a classified ad in France. The dog fetched the paper every morning.

"If I owned a chapel in Luxembourg would you marry me?" he said.

He made a bet with her that his dog could tune a piano. She lost, and went to breakfast with him. They took a table by the Eiffel Tower. He tried to look in her eyes. They had coffee and bagels, and talked about Italian Politics. He told her he sometimes felt like a criminal, she told him she sometimes knew the Chief of Police. The dog chewed on croissants. When she left he forced her to take his phone number.

She thought she would never call.

And she never did.

The Case of the Uncooperative Corpse

From the writings of Sgt. Woodrow Walsh, North West Mounted Police (Manitoba Provincial Archives)

IT WAS SPRING of 1904 in Winnipeg and that particular morning found us trying to keep the blood and coal dust from our boots. Not until the case was ended would we know the full and deep wickedness of the crime. But enough wickedness was immediately apparent. More than enough.

It was hardly our finest hour, or even one of our finer hours, but the investigation proved noteworthy in several aspects. Chiefly it entailed our encounter with Charles Kemper, as clever and resourceful and ruthless a blackguard as I have ever met.

We stood in the coal yard off Wardlaw Avenue just east of Osborne Street, which was now bustling with horse coaches, hansom cabs and streetcars. Men had started to arrive for work but none came within our vicinity. From their vantage point the prone feet could be seen sticking out from behind the coal pile but they were spared the rest. Our man had been shot in the chest, directly in the heart as it turned out, but more horribly several more shots had been fired close into his face, rendering him nearly without features. Blood soaked into the ground. The feet were splayed slightly, the hands held nothing.

Standing with me over that grisly corpse was Const. Powers. He had arrived from Ottawa only days before and this was the very first case to test our professional relationship. I knew very little of him. I knew he was good with a gun and never backed down from a fight, qualities which in his hands seemed to create as many problems as they solved. He was stationed for several years in Saskatchewan until the Massacre at Goose Rock, then was sent to British Columbia where he later figured prominently in the Outrage at Salmon Falls. He was finally transferred to Medicine Hat, Alberta where he fared no better, becoming a principal player in the Shootout at Cannibal Creek. While lacking finesse he was by no means without skills, so after some discussions with his uncle, a thoroughly reasonable man who at that time was occupied with a seat in Parliament, our superiors decided to transfer him somewhere he could develop into a more rounded officer. And so he came under my tutelage.

Winnipeg of course had its own police force, but the North West Mounted Police maintained a presence there to aid that department and provide service of a special nature.

Winnipeg was in these days a booming city of unending interest. I should say a city of many competing interests ranging from the innocent to the illicit. The gateway to the North and West, to the vast open spaces of a brash, young country, fortunes were being made and lost, new goods and people disgorged daily from the trains and the grain barons were all over raising their great buildings of stone and brick.

Commerce and a new century had made it a frontier town no longer, but it retained its rambunctiousness and encouraged feverish dreams. The city was home to French separatists, Irish Fenians, anarchists, Marxists, various labour agitators, occultists, Métis rabble-rousers, Chinese opium smugglers and secret societies too numerous to mention. The law had to contend with everything from Wild West bank robbery to espionage. My role was sleuthing, countering intrigue with intrigue, pulling at the threads of seemingly cleverly woven crimes.

There were some decent and capable men on the local force but on the whole our relationship with the city police was strained, the happy exception being Chief Edwin Cassells, who was a whist partner of mine many an evening at the Oak and Elm. It was he who summoned me.

The body had no wallet, no money, no rings and the clothes, worn but respectable enough, gave little indication who the wearer might be. Later in the day the bullets would be found, the ground shoveled up on my orders while two constables sifted through it like prospectors hunting for gold. I gently lifted the head, noted the damage and the ground, and eased it down.

"It occurred here, I believe," I said. "The body was not dumped." I looked around the yard, which would have been so desolate and lonely at night. "He was brought here or lured here."

Chief Cassells forced his gaze back onto the corpse. "Do you think that's to prevent anyone recognizing him? Or was it done in a fit of rage?"

"I'm unprepared to say."

"He was spotted by a night watchman. He assumed at first he was drunk."

Const. Powers, kneeling next to the body, said, "I hate a man who can't hold his bullets."

I stared at him. His expression betrayed nothing. Our long partnership was, I dare say, successful, as the newspapers can attest, but I must confess there was always something unreadable about the man. Something barely trustworthy even, though I would trust him with my life. My family name comes to me from Scotland, where my brothers and sisters have at times tasted the bitter taste of prejudice, so I am loathe to commit that offence, but I believed, then as now, that Powers' mother was a Galician. A Ruthenian Galician, to be fair. I hardly mind, but it's best to have things like that out in the open.

Const. Powers patted the inside of every pocket with great care and pulled a scrap of paper from the victim's coat.

"What is it?" I asked.

"A pay stub. Peter Halushko," he read aloud. "A labourer at Alexander Docks."

"Halushko? Sure he works here right enough. When he's not dead drunk which is a bit of an occasion. Doesn't shirk his load when he's here but that'd be two, sometimes three days a week. He's not here presently."

"We know," said Const. Powers.

I intervened. "Tell us what you know of him. His habits, his friends, anything that comes to mind."

"Is he in trouble?"

"Almost certainly."

"Well…" Halushko's employer rubbed his jaw. "He has money, he does. I mean, too much money. More than I pay him."

"Where does he get it?"

His employer smiled. "Ah, that I don't know. Why would I ask?"

He had an address for Halushko, God willing a real one, but not much else to aid us. We questioned the other workers as well and all said Halushko kept to himself. He had no friends. He confided nothing. He talked a little of gambling, but nothing very specific.

Halushko's address revealed itself to be a boarding house

of questionable reputation and cleanliness on Aikins Street. His room was next to an alley fire escape at the end of the hall, which he evidently used for he was hardly ever seen. He took his meals elsewhere. The landlady, after some reluctance and complaint, took us up to his room but stopped in front of it, looking from her key ring to the shiny lock on the door.

I was near to losing patience with her before realization dawned.

"Is that your lock?" I asked.

She shook her head.

I knocked and after receiving no answer put my shoulder to the door. While I rested it Const. Powers managed with some sustained effort to kick the door in. No one was there and, once the landlady was satisfied there was no fire and brimstone or communist meetings present, we sent her downstairs. Const. Powers surveyed the heavy lock more closely.

"Sturdy."

Pulling back the curtain I saw the window had half a dozen thick nails securing it shut. Const. Powers found a loaded pistol under the bed's pillow. Further search found some clothes, several old newspapers and eight hundred dollars in the mattress. Too much money indeed. There was nothing else except for one very peculiar thing, which Const. Powers drew my attention to. A small note tacked to the centre of one bare wall. All it read was, "Everywhere Danger."

I leaned in to study the note. "What have you been up to, Peter Halushko?"

The room's removable contents being secured at the James Avenue Police Station, Const. Powers and I retired to a nearby pub for our supper and to contemplate the mystery.

"What do you think, sir?"

"More than a little queer. That room. If it's robbery, he's beyond our reach I fear. But if there was another motive we may yet endeavour to draw the fiend out."

"Do you think it was one man then, sir?"

"It could have been one. It may have been several."

"But you have a plan?"

"We'll see. My thoughts need some settling. We'll meet at my office seven a.m. tomorrow to tackle this anew." I sent Const. Powers home and went to my own rooms on Balmoral Street, though I paid my bed barely a glance. My exploits it seemed were always garnering attention, but thankfully one aspect of my work escaped public praise. Now all these years later, it does no harm to reveal that I was a master of disguise. With just some ashes, tobacco juice and gum arabis, along with various contortions of the body or face, I might completely transform my appearance.

On this occasion, I added several decades of dissolute living to my countenance, stooped my frame, dressed in dirty rags, adopted a cane and filthy pipe and before long it was a doddering old man who unsteadily treaded down my back steps.

In my new incarnation as an aged member of the criminal class I set out for the rough and tumble saloons along Main Street. I wandered into a saloon appearing a little the worse for drink and announced, with perhaps too much volume and not enough tact, that I was looking for my friend Peter Halushko. I confided to those in my proximity that Peter had entrusted something to my safekeeping, something I no longer wished to be responsible for. Those around me looked at me with seeming indifference or disdain. I ordered a shot of rotgut brandy and downed it, secretly letting most of it dribble down my chin. Ignoring the unpleasant burning on my lips and chin, I leaned heavily on my cane, nearly falling, bid an exaggeratedly formal good evening and stepped back into the night. On to the next saloon where the whole performance was repeated again. And so on down the line, no one suspecting that the sad specimen before them was Sgt. Woodrow Walsh of the North West Mounted Police.

As you can no doubt guess I hoped to flush out some news or even tempt the evil behind this murder into action. It was not without risk, but duty is never a frivolous thing. It was after five or six stops that I managed to provoke a mild reaction. At the mention of Peter Halushko I drew the gaze of an old codger drinking by himself in the corner. He kept me in the corner of his eye, nothing too obvious, but I took note. He did not look in the best of health but I imagined real malevolence in his eyes. I decided to wait for him outside and follow him when he left, but to my surprise he pulled himself up and headed to the door after me. Careful to look the other way I slowed down my gait, giving him chance to follow. Stealing furtive glances I saw him lurch and limp down the street in my direction, one hand rubbing his hip. The old man had no easy time of it struggling to keep up, even with our molasses pace.

I was considering where I should lead him when I realized I no longer heard his shuffling feet. Glancing behind me I was startled to find him only a step away. I grabbed his wrist firmly but not roughly and was about to ask him some questions when his wrist wrenched free and his other hand grabbed my collar with lightning swiftness. This was no feeble old man. Lifted to my toes, he hurled me around and threw me against a building with more force than I could have expected. We were now in an unlit alley just off the road. His fist shot into my belly, leaving me gasping for breath. No longer slouching, he kicked one leg out from underneath me. He brought a fist down on the side of my neck, causing the night to go darker. I braced for the next vicious blow but none came. My assailant grunted and pitched forward. A tall figure stood behind him.

"Sir?"

Const. Powers had brought the butt of his gun down hard against the head of my attacker. Const. Powers kicked him in the midsection as he knelt on his hands and knees before us.

"Constable Powers. What are you doing here?'

"Couldn't sleep, sir."

It hardly seemed the circumstances to find fault with his impertinence. I reached out my hand and he helped me up. "Is our new suspect in the Land of Nod?"

"No." Const. Powers holstered his weapon under his plain-clothes and roughly threw the groaning man against the wall. Const. Powers was a tall, strapping lad who played hockey in the winter and cricket in the summer, and would later gain approving looks on the frozen rivers and on the cricket field in the soon-to-open Assiniboine Park.

"Stop," said my thwarted attacker.

"You don't want softening up?" said Const. Powers.

The man held up one hand. "Stop. Stop in the name of the North West Mounted Police."

That brought us pause, I can tell you.

"What was that?" I asked.

"I am a constable and you will explain yourselves."

"Do you take us for fools?"

"No, I take you for criminals soon headed for lockup."

"No jail in this city would take me. I am Sergeant Woodrow Walsh. This is my man Constable Powers." I gestured at my rags. "I am under disguise, but evidently I'm not the only one."

He saluted. "Constable James Everett, sir."

I carefully scrutinized the badge he produced to confirm its authenticity, which I considered prudent. He did likewise to mine.

"So what is the meaning of this?" I said.

"I am a spy. A secret agent in the criminal underworld. On a mission of utmost importance. Sir."

"So important I haven't been informed?"

"Your involvement has not been required, sir." Seeing me bristle he added, "The decision was made far above me, sir."

"Why did you follow me?"

"Why were you beating the bushes for Peter Halushko?"

"Why did you follow me?" I repeated, but Const. Everett's mouth stayed closed. Even the teeth behind seemed clamped shut. I sighed. "Do you know Halushko?"

Const. Everett considered me a moment. "You could say that. Yes."

"I'm sorry to tell you he's dead."

The shock was palpable. He looked from me to Const. Powers and back to me. "He can't be dead."

"I am sorry."

"I don't understand."

I have been the bearer of unbearable news many times over in my life but I never did lose my distaste for it. "I'm truly sorry. It's difficult I realize, but can you tell us what –"

"No, I mean really can't be dead. Actually impossible." He took a deep breath. "You see, I am Peter Halushko."

The pub was not quiet but the hour was late and most the patrons insensible. The three of us sat at a table in the corner, leaning over our watery pints of ale to talk the more privately. The light was poor, leaving the heavy wooden beams high above us but shadows. Const. Everett had his chair flat against the rough brick wall behind him. He rubbed the back of his head.

"Sorry," said Const. Powers.

"Quite all right. I would have done the same. In fact, more or less did."

"It was an ungentlemanly introduction, but I've had worse. Perhaps none so peculiar though," I said.

Const. Everett said nothing.

"We are investigating a murder so your secrecy be damned. What is it you're doing?"

He suddenly looked close to tears. "I'm alone, Sergeant. After all these many months my dreams are soaked in blood and sin and I don't know who to trust. But I know who you are, of course. I'll have to trust to that. Your reputation."

I waited for him to continue.

"Peter Halushko is my assumed identity. He's a rough and ready thug gaining friends in this town. He doesn't really exist. He never did." His voice lowered even further and we strained to hear. "I am gathering intelligence on the surviving active members of the Dead Shot Dogs."

At the mention of that name Const. Powers and I froze.

"You said active," said Const. Powers.

"Yes. Make no mistake. The gang has fallen on hard times but they are far from disbanded. But that's not the end of my task."

"No?" said I.

"No. I have insinuated myself into what's left of the criminal network to probe into the whereabouts of Vincent Apollo."

Vincent Apollo! That mastermind of murder and mayhem. A genius, a swashbuckler and a degenerate. My nemesis. He was, truth be told, considered by the public and most the papers to be Sgt. Sam Steele's nemesis, and I certainly can't argue that. But I considered him my nemesis as well, not without merit.

His whereabouts was a question much pondered. Was he up north? In the United States? Overseas, perhaps? No one knew.

Apollo had taken the reins of the Dead Shot Dogs in his bloody fist and made them into the terror of the 1890s. He made members of the weaker sex swoon and lured many foolish men to their downfall. English, French, Irish, Russian,

Slavic, he drew his loyal followers from all quarters and for a time held much of the West in his palm, with this city his pearl.

After the gang's disaster at the Trafalgar Warehouse in 1900 Apollo had disappeared. He was rumoured to be seriously wounded. He may or may not have been. He was too clever by half to show himself until his army of murderers, extortionists and robbers was strong again.

Const. Everett looked a man haunted. "His name is barely whispered but I believe he's safe somewhere. I believe he's coming back."

We let that troubling idea hover and settle. Then, it being our turn, we told him of the discovery of the corpse in the coal yard.

"But how did you come to think it was me? Or, I should say, Halushko?"

"There was a pay stub in the coat pocket," I said. He frowned.

"Do you have any idea how it could have got there?" said Const. Powers.

"I keep moving. A different place every night. But I keep a room at the Woodbine Hotel. No one's supposed to know about it, but it was ransacked a few nights ago."

We all three considered that. Then another question came to mind. "We were in your room. The one on Aikins Street."

Const. Everett seemed a little wary. "Yes?"

"We wondered about the note."

"The note?"

"On the wall. 'Everywhere Danger.' More than a little cryptic."

Const. Everett stared at us. "I didn't see a note."

I ordered another round.

Perhaps it was the second or third ale, but Const. Everett confided a little more, confessing the constant crime and danger was taking its toll. He had even committed crimes,

crimes which weighed heavily on his conscience and of which he would not speak. I told him I disapproved.

"But what am I to do?" he said. "My situation is most difficult. I must succeed. Yet I don't know how much longer I can last. My life or my sanity may be lost."

I did not envy him and said as much. We offered to help if we could.

"There is something. I was briefed on most of the Dead Shot Dogs associates. But I have recently gained the attention of rival gangs and face danger from that direction now as well. I am at a disadvantage. Do you have any files I could consult?"

"What I have is available to you."

"Do you have a file on Charlie Kemper?"

"Of course. But why?"

"It may be nothing. But it may help. The question is can we afford to risk another meeting?"

"In Chinatown. Tomorrow night. Find the Blue Dragon Tea House. I'll have a back room reserved for us. Ask for John B. Macdonald."

"Right. Till tomorrow night." He stood and left.

The merchants had brought in their carts and crates of exotic goods hours before but some of the strange scents lingered in the street. The faded signs in Chinese script were tinted red under the paper lanterns. A building with ascending levels of pagoda-style roofs towered into the sky, competing with the new Wentworth Building beside it with its ionic columns and its four gargoyles on each topmost corner. The curtains in the windows of the Blue Dragon Tea House were thick. The clientele was mostly but not entirely Oriental. The kind of place where opium seekers soon left disappointed, but where a man might walk to the back rooms without removing his hat and not generate suspicion or even curiosity.

Const. Everett shut the door behind him, throwing his hat on a chair.

"What's wrong?" said Const. Powers. He rose.

"Nothing. At least for the moment. I've spent the entire day on streetcars, horse coaches, in alleys."

"What happened?"

"A man was following me this morning. Or may have been. Perhaps I've gone paranoiac. A man in a bowler hat. Lord, I didn't like the looks of him. His eyes could cut steel."

Const. Powers and I exchanged looks. Neither of us liked the sound of that. "Perhaps it's time for your mission to come to an end. Where is your minder?" I said.

He seemed bitterly amused. "I drop off reports and pick up orders at prearranged places and times. Like a ransomer."

On what precipice had this young man been placed? "Come with me to Lower Fort Garry. You've done all you could and no one will dare ask for more."

"No, I can't. I'm so close to learning something about Apollo. I can sense it."

There was nothing more to say. We waited while Const. Everett poured over the files we had brought. His lips mumbled as he read as he clearly put great effort into committing as much as he could to memory. He looked at the Kemper file last.

"Nasty bit of business," I said.

"Hmm? Ah. Yes. Nasty. I dare say he's done even more evil than is catalogued here." His eyes returned to the file. "Two police officers dead in Berlin. One in Edmonton. And I fear there could be more."

He snapped the folder shut. "I must be away. If you need to reach me leave a message at the Woodbine. Ask for Wilfrid Laurier."

And with that he left. Const. Powers and I gathered up the papers and our coats and returned to my lodgings.

"I feel I'm swimming in dark water, sir. What now? We're short a victim's name and long on villains. I mean, Vincent Apollo?"

"It's no easy chestnut to crack. Why would someone want us to think Halushko is dead? Or did our victim have the pay stub for another reason? Confounding. I'll have to let Chief Cassells know the Dead Shot Dogs may be involved. We had hoped they would drift apart, foolishly perhaps. Const. Powers, we'll start again tomorrow, back at the coal yard." We were at my steps. He gave me a queer look.

"I won't find you on the street tonight disguised as a tee-totaler suffragette?"

It's my fault. Others have long noted, noted even in print, that over the long course of our partnership there was often a distinct lack of formality. A surplus of cheek. Here was the time to correct it, to administer an ounce of prevention with discipline. I blame myself.

I bid Const. Powers good night, a little too much amused and not enough chagrined. I put on my night robes and went to bed much troubled. For the first time I felt doubt about solving the case. The possibility of having to bury the victim before anyone knew who he was also gnawed at me. I felt only marginally better as I took my breakfast tea in my study.

There was a loud knock on the front door. I heard the urgent voice of my new protégé as the maidservant let him in. Without waiting for her he showed himself into the study. I stood up at seeing his expression.

"What is it?"

"We have an identification of the body, sir."

"She swears it's him." The coroner leaned against his desk Two city constables stood to the side.

"But how? How can she be sure?" I said.

The morgue was in the basement of the fortress on James Avenue, which also housed the police station and law courts. It was a little cool and dank, though well lit, and the coroner was usually fighting a cold.

"It's his mother." The coroner turned back to the paper on his desk. "He's been missing a week, or nearly."

"I just don't want to – "

The coroner interrupted me. "She swears she recognizes him, his hair, his teeth, his build. His hands. She even bought the clothes he was wearing. She says there's no doubt."

I shuddered to think of a mother having to look at her son in that condition. "Who is he?"

"Jack Duthee."

Jack Duthee was, to put it delicately, not on the social register. He was known to the city police, though never arrested, but even the most casual acquaintance could tell us Duthee had been an inveterate gambler. His work habits were also easy to discern. He had none. No regular employment.

We consulted with Chief Cassells and his men for several hours on Duthee and how his life may have reached its brutal end. Because of Const. Everett's tenuous position Const. Powers and I decided to not yet discuss that aspect of the investigation other than to say we spoke with Halushko. The pay stub, in any case, was as confusing to us as anyone else. Duthee's mother had provided a photo of her son, the poor, poor woman, and copies were ordered.

"They ruined his face and his heart," said Const. Powers, looking it over.

"Our victim has a name and soon we'll meet the killer," said I.

Outside the station Cummings, the reporter from the Tribune, hailed me.

"Walsh, how bout a personal warning or challenge to whoever did this murder on your turf?"

"I'm afraid not."

"C'mon, Walsh, something."

"Now that we have identified the unfortunate Mr. Jack Duthee we feel confident his habits, circumstances and associates will present logical and irrefutable evidence pointing towards the culprit or culprits."

Cummings, disappointed, wrote it down.

"It was bound to happen."

Alice, whose last name I will decline to mention here for the sake of propriety, was an ex-fiancé of Duthee's. The engagement had broken off more than a year before but perhaps the recriminations were still fresh. My confidence with the Tribune reporter notwithstanding, the investigation was not progressing as hoped.

"What does that mean, bound to happen?" said Const. Powers.

Alice shrugged.

Const. Powers persevered through eye rolls, sighs and now shrugs. "Did he owe you money?"

Her nostrils exhaled contempt. "Everyone but me."

"Tell me about his debts."

She gave an eye roll and sigh in tandem. "Of course he did not discuss them with me in any detail."

We soon took our leave.

"Well, he's dead, but at least he didn't marry her," said Const. Powers.

While I didn't disagree with the sentiment I was too frustrated for levity. Jack Duthee had gambling debts but they did not lead to strong suspects. We visited his haunts, made his regular gambling dens uncomfortable and talked to friends, family and neighbours to no avail.

At last though, some encouraging news came to me from one of my informers. His name was Gudmundsson, a strong drinker and weak gambler, a traveling tinsmith who took his trade up and down city streets in a pushcart, coming into contact with all manners of people. He was also a passable if unimpressive locksmith of ill repute. All of which made him a useful though not enthused agent of justice.

He left word where to find him at my lodgings and we met him on Simcoe Street, Const. Powers and I waiting on the steps of a friend of mine while Gudmundsson pushed his cart our way.

"Sigfus, how is the tin trade?"

"Not so good, not so good." He was an Icelander and had the disposition common to that glum race. "The money not so much. And my back. No good."

"This is Constable Powers, my new partner."

"My back. But no rest for me. Oh, no."

"What can you tell me, Sigfus?"

"I want reward. Not tea money."

"We'll see. You know something about Jack Duthee?"

"We'll see."

"Do you want to spend all your tea money on bail?"

"Fine, fine. No trouble. Duthee's friends the Spencer boys. Others."

"What about them?"

"They're at a house in Point Douglas. I was by. They don't leave. They don't go out. These boys. Some damn outfit."

"They don't leave the house? Not even for gambling?"

"Not for days."

The Spencer brothers not gambling was cause enough for suspicion. A thrill leapt through me to think justice could be close. "Any idea what they're up to?"

"Not so smart. Not so nice. Some damn outfit. They don't go out. They're hiding something. Guarding something. You be careful," he said, adding, "Tin business not so good."

The house was all shutters and shades, with no hint of what might be going on inside. It was several blocks removed from well-tread Annabella Street and so outside of Winnipeg's Red Light District which nestled in the bend of the Red River. It was nearly dusk and Const. Powers and I huddled with Chief Cassells and two of his best men, all of us hidden around the corner of the next-door house. We'd just converged on our spot and spoke in whispers.

"Up to half a dozen men in the house we estimate. What else who can say?" said Chief Cassells. "Sergeant Walsh, what do you deem our best course? Should we attempt to solicit their co-operation?"

"If they are connected to this ugly business they may respond poorly. Hide evidence of their crime or, dare I say, hide evidence of us. I think surprise is of the essence. Constable Powers, your thoughts?"

He strolled quickly up to the door, his gun out.

"Well, then." I sent Chief Cassells and his men around back and crept up the front steps.

Const. Powers gently turned the knob, shook his head. He wound up and kicked. The third kick sent the door flying inward and we burst into the room.

One of the Spencer brothers leapt off the chesterfield, much surprised. Const. Powers kicked him savagely in a region the Queensbury Rules strictly forbid.

"Wha?" uttered a man standing in the kitchen doorway, a bowl of porridge held close to his face, a spoon raised to his mouth.

Const. Powers hit him in the face with the butt of his gun, sending him and his bloody nose into the kitchen.

"Police!" I yelled.

We ran up the stairs as Chief Cassells and his men entered the room from the kitchen. We heard heavy footsteps and the slam of a door above. A man tried to run across the upstairs hall, from one room to another, but Const. Powers caught his hair. His head stopped, his feet kept moving out from under him. Const. Powers slammed his head into the doorframe and down he went. Another man disappeared through a doorway ahead and I ran past my colleague in pursuit.

"Police! Down on the floor!"

The man put himself on the floor with fervour. "I surrender! Please!"

I heard my name so handcuffed the suspect and returned to the hall where stood Const. Powers, Chief Cassells and his men.

"This is the only locked room," said Const. Powers.

This door was sturdier and resisted but after the other men took a turn Const. Powers tried again and wood cracked. Another splintering sound and the door opened. It was a large bedroom but sparsely furnished and plain. The window was now opened and the man looking out it turned to us when he heard the door finally give way. The hair rose on the back of my neck. He, for his part, looked no more at ease.

We all just stood still for a moment. My frightful shock quickly was replaced with mounting frustration. The others somehow retained their calm. I thought of days fruitlessly spent, the lack of progress, the cursed bewilderment of it all. I thought of that corpse as it lay behind the coal pile. So disrespected and offended against.

"Who are you?" But I knew.

"I'm Jack Duthee."

"We were informed you were dead," said Const. Powers.

"…Well, I'm not."

"Damnable nuisance, sir, damnable nuisance!"

Jack Duthee slumped in his chair at the station. His mother

sat in a cell nearby and he knew it. Police constables surrounded him and he could tangibly feel the lack of moral support.

"Didn't seem like no harm," he said in a low voice.

"You've interfered with a murder investigation. No, sabotaged it," I said.

"Didn't mean no harm."

"The body is buried. You realize that? Your mother buried the body. It's in Elmwood Cemetery, sacred ground. Before God. Under your name."

He looked close to tears.

"We took up a collection among the lads. We helped pay for the bloody tombstone," said Chief Cassells.

"I'm sorry."

Const. Powers leaned against the wall, his arms crossed. "If we kill him before New Year's he can still use it."

Chief Cassells and I decided not to disturb the corpse for the time being. With confessions in hand from Jack Duthee and Mrs. Duthee, Chief Cassells went that same night to see the crown attorney. The story was Duthee was given a large sum of money to settle most of his debts. He'd spent a large portion in days without any benefit to his creditors. His former fiancé gained a little understanding from me. Mrs. Duthee also shared the good fortune. In return, Duthee was to leave town, to pretend he was dead. His mother reported him missing and identified the corpse as her son. They would not or could not give anything but a vague description of the man who hired them. Average sort of fellow. With a bowler hat.

Const. Powers and I could not help but feel like Napoleon with Wellesley on his flank. Much discouraged and apprehensive we questioned the Duthees' neighbours the next morning. We spoke to the coroner again as well, but it seemed no use. Leaving the station Cummings appeared at my side.

"Well, J——, Walsh, you make a fellow look bad."

"What are we to do? We had a mother grieving for her son."

"It makes a fellow look bad. A dead guy not being dead? It creates a… a credibility quandary. If people can't trust what they read in the paper they'll start getting their news from the Bible again. I mean, dead and not dead, we're mixing up two opposites here."

"Cummings, a man is dead."

"Are you sure?"

I turned on him. "This is proving a taxing case. Justice and order depend on us, demand our best efforts. So I care not one whit about your quandaries!"

"Don't be sore, Walsh. It makes a fellow look bad is all I'm saying."

I sat on a bench in Market Square, elbows on knees and hands propped under my chin, looking out over the small lawn. The tall warehouses of King Street loomed behind us. Before us was the Leland Hotel with its famous baths and arched entrance, the Ashdown Building with its faux Egyptian sphinx and beyond those on the other side of Main Street was the Alexandria with its Gothic tower piercing the sky. Visual marvels all, signs of unbridled imagination and optimism. Const. Powers sat on the other end of the bench.

"I am at a bit of a loss," I said.

It was a long pause before he spoke. "Sir, that pay stub was planted for a reason. We were meant to think the victim was Halushko. Why? I have no idea, but it's tied into Everett's mission somehow. Then there's the man with the bowler hat."

"Yes, the man with the bowler bothers me. As for Const.

Everett's work, I agree."

"I think Everett is in danger. And I'm not sure if he's told us everything."

The mention of danger made me think of the note in Const. Everett's room. Of that locked and fastened room and who could have gained entrance at will and without detection. Thoughts uncomfortable enough that I looked over both shoulders.

"Why fake Halushko/Everett's death?" I said. "To collect some sort of bounty? Unlikely. Perhaps an attempt to spirit him away without anyone knowing?" For torture, I did not say.

"Whatever the case, I propose we go to the Woodbine. If Everett's not there let's go to headquarters. His reports are going to somebody there."

"Good thinking, Daniel." I stood up. "Shed some light on Constable Everett's work and we'll shed some light on our mystery."

We stepped into the Woodbine Hotel. It was doing a bustling business but hardly looked crowded. The establishment's recently finished bar, soon to be world-renowned, was the longest on the continent. Its finely polished wood counter stretched into the distance. I hadn't had such an unimpeded view of it before and had to admit it was impressive. You'd be hard pressed to knock a cricket ball down the entire length of it. But Everett was neither there or in his room, nor did we expect it. We left a note for him and headed for the police stables, forgoing a horse coach or hansom cab. Riding horses north up Main Street and out of the city we arrived in scarcely an hour at Lower Fort Garry, division D headquarters of the North West Mounted Police.

The sight always made my heart sing. The first headquarters

of our force, its largest training academy and the centre from which the West's peace and order emanated. Its flags flew high in the breeze. The outer wall was a chest-high wooden fence and through its many guarded gates there was much traffic of messengers and constables. Inside there were many large tents and some small, and in the distance cadets were being shouted through horse drills. We came to the fort proper with its thick stone and mortar walls and its low turrets. We dismounted at the main gate and, myself being recognized, the constables showed us in.

We stabled our mounts and presented ourselves at the antechamber of Colonel Hugh Bracebridge, commissioner of D division. We stated our business and hoped to avoid a long wait but at the mention of Const. James Everett Col. Bracebridge's assistant brought us in to him almost at once. He was standing at his expansive rosewood desk with one of his trusted advisors, Major McFayden.

"You've seen Everett? You've spoken with him?" said Col. Bracebridge.

"Yes, sir, Commissioner."

"Tell us, Sergeant Walsh. Omit nothing."

I outlined our two meetings with Const. Everett and everything that was said, and they started at Everett's request to see the Kemper file. I then brought them up to date on the murder investigation and its poor state, which I sadly admit stung my pride.

"Sergeant, we've lost contact with Everett for several days now. Since before you saw him."

"His position seems precarious, sir. He did mention that man following him," I said. "Respectfully, sir, there's much Constable Everett didn't tell us. Constable Powers and I feel his clandestine activities likely have significant bearing on this strange murder."

"I'm afraid that's entirely possible," said Col. Bracebridge. "I hardly need say this conversation shan't escape this office?"

"No, sir," said I.

"No, sir," repeated Const. Powers.

Col. Bracebridge confirmed that Const. Everett was working to undermine the Dead Shot Dogs and learn if he could the whereabouts of Vincent Apollo. For eight long, harrowing months he'd laboured to bring his false identity under the confidence of the gang.

"What's more, he has met with success. Several months ago he managed to recruit a spy."

"A spy, sir?" I said.

"A member of the Dead Shot Dogs has turned informer. We were skeptical at first, but his information has proven valuable. Very valuable."

I remembered recent headlines. "Riley?"

"Yes, Joe Riley. Apollo's poisoner. When he hangs, the country will breathe a little easier. Certainly eat and drink a little easier. His capture in Port Arthur came from information passed on to us from Everett's spy."

"Who is this spy?"

"We don't know," said Maj. McFayden.

"Everett would not identify him, not even to us," said Col. Bracebridge. "His reports give no clue. Thank God."

"Yes. There has been a very disturbing development," said Maj. McFayden. He seemed reluctant to say more.

"Sir?"

"It seems we've had a breach. A breach of our files in our Ottawa headquarters," said Col. Bracebridge. "We were as shocked as you. The further outrage is it could only have been one of our own members. The devil take him when we get our hands on him. Just over a week ago a locked cabinet was found open. No papers were missing but it's believed some of Everett's reports were seen."

"Luckily, Everett's other identity of Halushko was never written down," said Maj. McFayden. "Only the commissioner and I knew it, and now you."

"And Everett wouldn't reveal his spy to anyone, in writing or in person," said Col. Bracebridge. "Even so, we wrestled with cancelling the mission. Then resolved to. We got word days ago that it's believed Charles Kemper has come to Winnipeg to deal with both Everett and the informer. Kemper is one of Apollo's most dangerous men."

"He's escaped from prison three times. He's a cold blooded killer," said Maj. McFayden. "We gave the order at once for Everett to quit the mission."

"Only now we can't reach him," said Col Bracebridge. "It's imperative you find Everett and bring him in. His informer too, if possible."

"The informer was paid?" I asked.

"About five hundred dollars over several months, plus the two thousand dollar reward for Riley," said Col Bracebridge.

"I'll need the dates of those payments."

"You'll have them in moments. Maj. McFayden, see that their horses are readied."

We rode hard into town but before tackling the task in mind I went to Chief Cassells' office. I knew he had the list I wanted. Chief Cassells sat at his desk with a newspaper open in front of him. He looked up.

"Woodrow, did you actually tell a reporter this case has taxed all your modest wits?"

I had no time for that hogwash. I consulted his business registry and made a list of city banks.

"We'll hire a hansom cab. If we rode horses up to banks like the devil's at our heels people will think there's a robbery. Not very discreet."

"What are we doing, sir?" said Const. Powers.

"We're looking for one of two things. Either a bank account that has deposits on the days our informer received monies

– unlikely – or a deposit box that has been visited on those same days. It will be under a false name, I don't doubt, but our informer may have used a bank. It's a considerable amount of money. And it's money he can't explain should his associates stumble across it."

It took some persuasion to get most bank managers to allow to us to check dates for deposits and safety box visits. While Const. Powers frowned or glared, I explained the gravity of the situation, mixing in some flattery and gratitude of the entire force, until we had the information we needed. I believe the Dominion Bank on McDermot Avenue was our eighth. It had a deposit box which when checked against our dates matched up very nearly. I asked if we could see its contents.

"I'm afraid that's impossible," said the bank manager.

"Isn't there anything you can do?"

"Impossible?" said Const. Powers.

"Yes."

"Open it."

"No."

"Open the box."

"I really can't."

"What if it's a bomb?"

"Is it a bomb?"

"It could be a bomb."

"It's not a bomb."

I intervened. "No, it's not a bomb."

"Then I can't open it."

I tried a different tack. "Sir, it's not a bomb. We hope. But it might not be anything you'd want in your bank. You wouldn't just be aiding the police, you would be protecting all these other boxes here."

"Well…"

I gestured at the locked boxes in the walls. "For the greater good."

He opened the box. It contained fourteen hundred and thirty dollars, a gun and ammunition.

"Gold," said Const. Powers, meaning we'd struck gold.

We set up a snare for our informer. Opting against an elaborate disguise I merely stayed hid in the manager's office. He would signal to me if the man came in and I would follow him outside, where Const. Powers waited across the street. Two days we waited then our prayers were answered. A man with a hat pulled low entered and the manager signaled. When the man came out of the deposit box room I got a better look. I recognized the man.

Exiting the bank I waited a dozen steps before I grabbed the man's elbow. He shoved at me and reached into his pocket.

Const. Powers whacked him over the head with the butt of his gun, grabbed him by his jacket and threw him headlong into an alley.

The man fell to his knees and retched. He stopped, spat, and retched again.

Powers shrugged at me, confused.

"He thinks he's about to be murdered," I said.

I kneeled near to the man. "Gordon Peech."

His chest stopped heaving.

"Gordon Peech, I am Sergeant Woodrow Walsh and this is Constable Powers." I picked up his hat. "It's good to make your acquaintance."

It was dark and warm and loud. Everything rattled, like the whole world was being shook loose. Peech was still breathing heavily, trying to collect himself. Const. Powers and I sat across from him. Peech was a Dead Shot Dog of long standing. A forger but also a gunman. He played violin competently and spent most his money chasing barmaids and music hall girls. It was said he once killed a man over cards in Plum Coulee. Const. Powers presently held his pistol and knife for safekeeping.

I'd found a private horse coach, one with thick curtains, and brought it to the alley, then ordered the driver to keep moving. It was private but stuffy inside, and the coach clattered considerably.

"How do I know you're really police?"

"Because you're not dead," said Const. Powers.

He seemed to consider that. He looked us both over as the coach rounded a corner. "What do you want?"

"Constable Everett," I said.

"Who?" But his whole body trembled.

"Halushko."

"What?"

"Don't trifle with us. We're on your side."

"Not on your side exactly. But on a side that's not trying to kill you," said Const. Powers.

"Constable Everett. Where is he?"

"I don't know."

"We have some bad news for you," I said. "The Dead Shot Dogs know they have an informer in their ranks."

"What?" He visibly paled, even in this poor light. He cursed. "How?"

"A lapse in our vigilance. A spy in Ottawa saw the reports."

"Sorry about that," said Const. Powers.

"I'm afraid it gets worse. Charles Kemper was sent here."

Peech took a deep breath and softly knocked his head against the wall behind him. He slowly exhaled.

"You didn't know?" I said.

"No. But it's not just me. I don't think many of us know."

"We need to find Constable Everett. I recommend you come with us as well. The North West Mounted Police will aid your flight."

"But they don't know who it is, right? I could just go back

to my old life."

"Inadvisable. But that is your own affair." Not entirely true. "But until we find Constable Everett consider us your personal guard. How do you two set up your meets?"

"He decides. Our next meeting is in three nights." He took out a train ticket. "He gave me this. We both have tickets to a private compartment on the Moonlight Express. You know it?"

"Yes." Evening trains in the summertime to Winnipeg Beach on Lake Winnipeg. There was a new boardwalk on the beach and a large dance hall that was gaining popularity. There was a resort hotel but most took the train there and back the same night. I took the ticket and committed the compartment number to memory.

"What now?" said Peech.

I leaned out the window towards our driver. "The Calidore Hotel."

I looked down on the darkening street. There was no activity. I could not see them but I knew seraphs and cherubs floated about our window in stone relief, keeping the outside at bay and weeping at this world.

We no longer went out. Our note at the Woodbine had not been picked up. Outside the light was dying. Const. Powers and Peech each sat on one of the beds, Const. Powers with his back against the wall and his holster resting next to him.

"Is he coming back?" he said.

"Who?"

"You know who."

I sat in a chair. Peech answered. "He won't stay gone. It's not his nature."

"Do you know where Vincent Apollo is?" said Const. Powers.

"No."

"But you've met him? You know him?"

"Yes."

"What's he like?"

"He's like no one else." It seemed to be his whole answer but then he continued. "Do you read your history? Do you know Spartacus? He's like Spartacus with a gun."

He stared into space. "If he finds out what I've done he'll feed me alive to his dogs."

He laid down and pulled a blanket over himself as he turned to the wall and would say nothing else.

Const. Powers and I walked up the front steps of the grand Union Station, a reluctant Peech between us. There was little traffic on Main Street and we expected the station to be quiet. It was too early in the season for the Moonlight Express to have many passengers.

The building itself was long and narrow but at its centre was the large dome of the station's cavernous lobby. Its kaleidoscope of colours in stained glass tinted the marble floors far below. To the left and right of the dome the lobby was punctuated with marble pillars.

Peech darted looks left and right, occasionally glancing behind him. Const. Powers kept one hand on Peech's elbow and looked around more slowly. I was impatient to find our train but then to my great relief I spotted Const. Everett ahead of us, coming out of the public lavatory.

I whistled and raised my hand.

Just at that moment Peech yelled, "Kemper."

"Where?" I looked about.

A wolfish grin spread across Const. Everett's face. He yanked out his gun and started firing at us. A bullet hit Peech in his lower side. Another disturbed the brim of my hat.

Const. Powers shoved Peech, sending him skidding along the floor, and tackled me from behind. He landed on top of me, and before I could catch breath his gun was firing in his hand.

Our confusion was complete, but then a flood of insight forced me to face the horrible truth. Our mysterious corpse was Const. James Everett. The real Everett. The man we knew as Everett was Charles Kemper. Kemper, at gunpoint, had taken Const. Everett's belongings, his wallet, his badge and his train ticket. But he missed the pay stub in his coat pocket. Const. Everett wouldn't reveal his informer, even on pain of death, but Kemper guessed the ticket was for their next rendezvous. He killed that brave constable and shot him in the face as he lay on the ground. For if word got out of Everett's death, or even his alias Halushko's death, it could have scared away the informer. It was imperative Kemper hide his victim's identity, at least until the rendezvous. When he found me investigating Halushko's murder, he'd struck upon a brilliant and cold blooded ploy: to take on Const. Everett's identity. To complete his misdirection he arranged to have another man disappear for a while and be identified as his victim. The note in the real Everett's room was in his own handwriting. He'd written it as a constant caution to himself. Kemper didn't know about it because he'd never been in the room, had never even known its location.

But I digress.

Two men or more with guns ran up from behind Kemper. Const. Powers kneeled, his side turned to our attackers, and kept firing. He hit Kemper somewhere in the arm, causing him to yelp as his gun clattered to the ground. That discouraged his men's advance and gave us time to run for cover. Peech hid behind a pillar, screaming and clutching his side. He paused only to hurl curses at us. What innocent bystanders there were ran screaming or huddled along the ground.

Const. Powers and I ducked behind adjacent pillars. I pulled out my gun as he fired at Kemper, exasperated to say the least.

"What in Hell?" he yelled.

"He's Kemper."

"What?"

"That's Kemper."

It sunk in. "Damn."

Loud cracks echoed through the lobby. Const. Powers glanced around his pillar as shots ricocheted off it.

"Knucklebusters," he said, referring to the Winchester pump action rifles two of the men were using. Using with much enthusiasm.

Const. Powers now had Peech's gun in his other hand and ran to another pillar, firing both guns. He caught a man unexpectedly in the open. The bullet smashed the gunman's brain and down he went, his Winchester beyond his power. Blood pooled out over the marble floor.

Peech still screamed. I called out for Kemper to surrender. Bullets were the only reply. Men tried to get around us. I steeled my nerves and ran to another pillar. I fired my gun until it was empty and reloaded. Two more men came in, this time through the front doors, and panic threatened.

It was the nefarious Ranjan Sin, Apollo's Hindoo assassin. We had never met but there was no mistaking him. By reputation he sometimes wore a turban and garb oriental in appearance, sometimes was all in black and sometimes was dressed as he now was, in a white suit and straw boater hat. He was sharp with a gun but it was his knives that gave men nightmares. Those blades had sent many men to their grave. I also recognized the murderer Legrace, having run into him years ago in Portage la Prairie.

I fired in that direction and Const. Powers looked their way in time to see them find cover.

"That's Ranjan Sin?"

"It must be," I said.

"Damn."

Another shot bounced off my pillar. The fact that not one wayward, skyward bullet destroyed any of the magnificent glass of that great dome above us is something I thank heaven for to this day.

There was silence for a moment. Const. Powers began reloading his gun. Peech's gun was discarded, now useless to him. Const. Powers was nearly reloaded when, to my horror, a blade materialized in his shoulder.

Ranjan Sin charged. He came with another blade held low, ready to fillet him, and Const. Powers reached out both hands to stop his cobra-like strike at the wrist. The blade stopped short but Ranjan Sin put his weight behind it and it pierced Const. Powers' coat. He shouted and brought his knee to Ranjan Sin's groin.

Ranjan Sin avoided the worst of the blow but he was off balance and Const. Powers grabbed his head and smacked it against the pillar. He pulled the blade out of his shoulder and swept it across Ranjan Sin's chest, drawing blood.

Ranjan Sin did a stunning back flip, his foot just catching Const. Powers' chin. Const. Powers gave his head a small shake and they circled round each other, their blades in front of them. Const. Powers, the mad boy, deliberately stepped on Ranjan Sin's straw hat. Ranjan Sin smiled.

I was forced to return fire on the other men and when next I looked their way the two were locked in each other's grip, each free hand around the other's wrist. They pushed and pulled at each other and tried to bring their blades in. Const. Powers tried to butt him with his head but Ranjan Sin moved out of the way. Ranjan Sin brought his blade in a little closer and Const. Powers bit his finger. He dropped the blade but wrenched himself away. Smiling again, he pulled out another blade and lunged. Const. Powers leapt back then lunged himself.

I ran to another pillar, closer to Const. Powers, and it nearly cost me my life. In fact, I pretended it did and fell on my belly with my gun underneath me. I made myself count to eight, surely the longest eight seconds of my life, and twisted to one side as I brought up my gun.

A man, the one with the other Winchester, fired at me but the shot glanced off the floor next to me. I hit him in the chest and fired three more rounds with more deliberate aim. The bullets punched through him and he fell backwards against a pillar, streaking it with blood as he slumped to the floor. I wondered how many more were left. Three perhaps, but possibly up to five.

I shouted at Ranjan Sin he was under arrest. Const. Powers, his chest heaving, turned and leapt for his gun. Ranjan Sin hurled his knife at his back. The aim was true but the angle was poor and the blade did not stick. Const. Powers jumped up with his gun and fired. Ranjan Sin fell. Const. Powers sat down with his back to a pillar.

No death should be celebrated but the demise of Ranjan Sin would cause sighs of relief around the world, most especially in those places police officers gathered.

"Kemper!" More shots rang out. It was Peech, and he'd plucked the bloody Winchester from the pool of blood around the man Const. Powers had shot. "You're the man? You're taking me to the woodshed? Where's Apollo?"

He walked in a wide circle around the area Kemper seemed to be, shooting, stopping to curse at us a moment before taunting Kemper again. The rifle cracked, someone shot back at him.

I began to reload my gun with the last of my bullets. It was then I witnessed something to make me question my eyes. Now all these years later I wonder, but I know what I thought I saw. Ranjan Sin suddenly sat up, blinked and looked at me. He smiled and slowly held his bloody fist out to his side. Relaxing his grip he let a bullet fall out of his fist and clink to the floor. Then he scrambled up and ran.

I ran to Const. Powers, who was peering around his pillar. He saw Ranjan Sin's body missing.

"What?"

"He's gone. I don't know how."

"Damn."

I looked at my young protégé and felt my throat constrict. "Daniel, are you all right?" He'd suffered several cuts to his arms and torso, two or three of them quite deep. Blood spattered his coat and trickled down the fingers of one hand.

"I could use a bath, sir."

A woman's shriek tore the air.

"Walsh! She dies! She dies!"

Kemper had a young woman by the throat and a gun to her head. Her eyes were wide with pure terror and he held her close in front of him. I moved away from Const. Powers but kept my distance from Kemper. I had my gun on him but did not dare fire. Peech was nowhere to be seen.

Kemper began walking backwards with his hostage. "Where's Powers?"

"Dead, I think."

He seemed pleased with that. I kept step with him but veered a little to the right, forcing Kemper to turn his shoulders slightly to face me. Const. Powers skirted along the edges of the lobby behind him. I lost sight of him.

"Kemper, let her go. I won't shoot."

"I won't hang. Put down your gun."

I angled my nozzle off him but did not put it down. The woman whimpered.

"I want a horse." His back hit a pillar.

"All right."

"You think I'm a fool?"

"No." He was many things but not that.

Kemper sneered. "Sergeant Walsh gets his man. Saves the day. Think you'll save her?"

Const. Powers appeared, placed his gun to Kemper's temple and fired. Blood sprayed up and Kemper fell to the floor. Const. Powers gathered the girl and turned her to his chest, away from the sight. She clamped her arms around him and sobbed into his shoulder. There was the footsteps of fleeing men.

An ugly end to one of the worst Dead Shot Dogs to ever live.

"Sir!"

There was a flash of white out the doors.

We ran out the front doors. I heard the whinny of agitated horses. A coach sped away.

Const. Powers and I rushed down to the street where two bodies lay at the bottom of the steps. A coach driver stared up wide eyed at the broad evening sky, his neck snapped, one of his heels lying in the gutter at the curb, his skin still ruddy but the surprise and incomprehension in his face already cold. Gordon Peech sprawled out headfirst down the steps, on his back, his mouth open, the handle of a blade protruding from his chest.

Mischief Point

HIS FEET LEFT the floor of the boat and panic tightened his fingers' grip just in time, kept him out of sky and dark water. The impact of the next wave threw the aluminum bottom up at him before he had his footing back and he smacked both his knees. Pain jolted. Water spray fell over him as they hit the next wave and he pulled himself up.

Behind the wheel, standing with apparent ease, Snorri Hallgrimsson seemed not to notice the trouble. Not till his companion was back up. "Watch yourself," he said.

Cal McKay said nothing, went back to his half-standing, half-sitting crouch. He reached out for the lone oar, moved it out of the way, was disappointed with its very light heft.

"Snorri, is this safe?" More spray came over the windshield and dampened his hair.

"Yah. I guess so would think." Now in the open water of Lake Winnipeg, the swells were six feet high. The boat was a 20-footer, open-hulled, a commercial fishing boat built specifically with this lake in mind. It wouldn't be defeated by these swells, but with Snorri running the hell out of the 200 horsepower, and the boat aimed straight into the wind at 50 klicks an hour, it was a rough ride. An empty cooler bounced and banged around the front of the boat like it was full of live firecrackers.

Louder even than the howling wind was the crash of boat and water. It had a quick and regular rhythm, sounded to Cal's surprise very much like the clacking wheels of a train. Talking was not easy. But Cal fought to be heard. Talking was part of his plan.

"Snorri, why did we come out in this?" The sky was mostly blue but winds were high. Twenty knots? Less? More? To the north low grey clouds lay on the horizon.

"The lake makes you tough," said Snorri.

Cal looked at the distant shoreline, its crags, bays, points and islands an unintelligible smudge of green, a palette of black spruce, jack pine and trembling aspen.

"Where's Wicked Point?"

"See there?" Snorri pointed. "Not there. Behind there."

Any fisherman would know Wicked Point, could name each island they passed. But Snorri didn't hire fishermen. No Icelanders. Ever. No one with experience on the lake. He hired his help in the city.

Cal's eyes scanned the coast again, trying to distinguish one point from another. Like words in another language, he thought. He returned his gaze to inside the boat, taking inventory. He kicked the lockbox attached to the bottom that doubled as a bench. "What do you keep in here?"

"My important papers."

Cal laughed.

A larger wave crashed. Snorri angled the boat directly into the next few, then veered slightly away from shore. Cal wasn't sure he wasn't making it more difficult than it had to be.

Another wave and the prow looked to be inches away from digging in. Even Snorri's legs buckled a little to accommodate the bucking boat. He smiled. An old fisherman's smile, sometimes satisfied, sometimes fatalistic, almost hidden in creases of skin.

"A Nor'wester. A fish wind."

"A fish wind?"

"It brings the fish. Good fishing tomorrow."

"Always good fishing for you though, eh Snorri?"

Snorri said nothing. A king and his treasure. He brought in the best pickerel in the lake. Always had. The 'freshest fish' he would say. Others said it was like the whole fish was made of pickerel cheeks. And his favourite spot was productive. Snorri could fish his license in three weeks. And that was just the fish going through the Freshwater Fish Marketing Corporation. He sold more fish through the black market in Gimli. A wedding social or Thursday night at the Legion you could often buy a raffle ticket for ten or fifteen pounds of 'Snorri's fish.' No one had to ask which Snorri. A restaurant had once served his fish to a film crew shooting a movie in Gimli, and now the producer had it shipped to him in L.A. three times a year. Many had wondered over the years, but no one had learned the secret of his fish.

"How many nets do you keep?" said Cal.

"Twelve. Not so many."

"Must know what you're doing."

"I guess so would think."

"Why you do it? Fish?"

"No boss. Only the lake is boss. Fresh air. Hard work for good money." He gestured round, to the view, Cal supposed. "You have this every day. Also, I think it is in the blood."

Cal knew. Knew more than he said. His mother was a Gunnarsson.

"No other boats," said Cal. He was pleased, just as he was when they shipped out of Gimli harbour without being noticed. Good luck, he thought, not knowing Snorri only ever headed out to his fishing camp except in very bad weather.

Whitecaps grew on the swells. The grey clouds, still low, were closer.

"We should be OK," said Snorri, said it like he could be wrong but it didn't concern him much.

Cal had hardly ever been on the lake, but heard the stories from the time he was a child lying on the living room carpet, his uncles sprawled about with their cases of beer. A beautiful lake, but dangerous. "It's long and narrow and shallow and the wind runs right down the middle of it like a bitch," said his Uncle Kris.

Feigning ignorance, radiating his best innocence, Cal spoke up. "I looked up some maps. Just before I came out. But I couldn't find any Mischief Point."

Snorri pulled his gaze away from his driving to Cal. His expression unreadable behind skin cured and crinkled by sun and wind. "No?"

"No. Is it only on old maps?" Cal counted waves against the hull

"It's not on any maps. It was named by my grandfather and his brother," Snorri continued. "They had a camp on one of these little islands. My grandfather's brother went back to the mainland for supplies. Well, for more beer. His boat ran out of gas."

"Really?" Cal said to show concern.

"Yah. He drifted for two days, almost. Very lucky. He didn't have a life jacket. Not him, not in those days. He washed up on shore, on a little point. Tried a few nets in a little bay, because he was always scouting for fish."

"How'd he get home?" Lead him away and then back to it, he thought.

"Walked through the bush. But he got his bearings first, named the point."

"And that's how you found your secret spot."

"The spot's not the secret."

"What?"

"The spot's not the fish's secret."

Cal asked again but Snorri shrugged, concentrated on the water ahead of them again.

"And nobody knows where Mischief Point is but your family?"

Snorri seemed not to hear. Half an hour passed, Cal occupied with staying on his feet, not busting his nose on the top edge of the windshield.

Snorri pointed. "Wicked Point."

"Why Wicked?"

"Bad currents."

Cal thought he could tell Snorri a few things about wickedness. More wickedness than you could find on a boat. Four months out of Stony Mountain Penitentiary and Cal still had trouble sleeping.

Snorri shifted the motor down a little, a concession to the waves. "We want to pass here now. Soon it will be worse. The wind, see it's picking up?"

Cal pulled up his sleeve, angled his wrist, pushed a button. It was a bulky watch with its own global positioning system. Cal committed a few numbers to memory and pulled his sleeve down.

"Nice watch," said Snorri.

Cal nodded. He'd bought a cheaper GPS than he was supposed to, used or stolen, maybe. Kept the rest of the money. The Sigurdssons weren't paying him much, all things considered. He'd argued for more, knew it was pointless, and after pausing just long enough to soothe his dignity pulled his chair in close as everything was explained to him.

He wished now he'd just walked away. A rough fish. But not on anyone's hook. Cal looked around. He wasn't superstitious, but had a thought, hoped his bad luck couldn't follow him out on a boat. Leave that damn luck wandering the shore till it hit someone else.

The boat's motor cut out. Almost immediately the boat

pivoted, offering its broadside to the malevolent swells, rocking back and forth, starboard to port. Cal relaxed his grip, wriggled his fingers to get the blood flowing again. He gave himself a few seconds to drain the panic from his voice.

"We fucked, Snorri?"

Snorri looked confused. "Hmm? Ah. No. Gas." He began switching the empty tank for a full one.

The clouds were on them now. Cal stood straight up, stretched his legs.

"Those nets over there?"

Snorri looked, nodded. "Yah."

"They gonna catch much there?"

Snorri shrugged. "A man hopes. The fishing is good around here. It's not so much known for dancing and parties."

Cal laughed. "No? Maybe we should bring out some girls next time. What do you think?"

"Girlfriends are better on shore." He started up the motor again, righted the boat.

"Girlfriends? You have girlfriends, Snorri?" Cal teased, but not with any malice.

"A few."

Cal chortled. "A few? Snorri, you dog! Where are these girls?"

"Gimli. Winnipeg."

"You're kidding me." He digested the information. "Where you find these girlfriends?"

"The internet."

Cal shook his head, bemused. "The fuckin' internet."

A sense of – not affection – but camaraderie had crept up on Cal. He was regretting ever having stepped foot in the boat. Add it to the list, he thought.

He didn't feel like finding Snorri's spot. In town, over a drink, it felt like it would be an accomplishment. After all, others had looked for it over the years and no one had ever found it. A few even disappeared looking for it, not to be seen again. Probably because they were following the crazy old man into evil weather like this.

Snorri turned, studied the shore. There was a glimpse of a shack among the trees.

"What's that?"

"My camp," said Snorri. It wasn't much to look at from the water, but it was a one-man fishing camp with a broken sofa, a radio and a diesel generator that ran 24 hours a day through the fishing season. In back there was an ice-maker, refrigerated room for the tubs of fish and a tire-rutted track into the bush.

"Nice." He couldn't see much, but didn't think much of it. Cal checked his watch.

Soon they rounded another jut of land and were back in more unsheltered water. "We're not going very fast," said Snorri after several minutes. By Cal's reckoning they had been out for three hours. The pounding waves, even the mild fear that had settled in him when the boat left shore, now felt monotonous. Cal's thoughts wandered. Fishing had never seemed very tempting to him, but maybe he should have tried it, got on with one of his uncles. Made a go of it. Maybe things would have been better. At least one or two people would be happier. But he didn't want to think about that.

"Snorri, you ever do anything other than fish?"

"Not much."

"How do you know there wasn't a better job for you out there?"

"Like what?"

"I don't know. Farming?"

Snorri snorted dismissively.

"Well, I don't know, how bout own a bar or something?"

"I own a bar."

"What?"

"On number seven. My brother runs it."

"Really? And you're out here?"

Snorri shrugged.

"How long you been doing this?"

Snorri's head tilted. "Forty years or so."

"Fishing is your thing." Cal paused, could have been counting to forty. "I think I would be good at something."

Cal looked out over the waves, fantasized about going back to the Sigurdssons and laying a beating on them, telling them to leave an old man alone, then sitting down with a couple people and just settling some shit, and getting his girlfriend back, making love again in that attic apartment, Christmas lights slung over her Value Village bookcase and dresser.

But he knew the world wasn't like that and neither was he.

Cal pulled his coat tighter around his neck, worked the collar loose from the life jacket he was wearing. "How much damn further are we going?"

No answer.

"Hey! Where the hell is this place?"

Snorri said nothing. All emotion concealed by considerable stubbornness.

"I don't care about your damn secret spot, Snorri."

"The spot's not the secret."

"Right." He pushed down a flash of temper. Put his hands inside his coat for warmth. Felt the filleting knife in his pocket. He'd wanted to use the oar, but gave up on that, it felt like balsa wood. He ran his fingers over the knife handle. He imagined practiced gestures and moves with the handle, trying not to think of the consequences of the blade. God made fish and fishermen and pretty much left them to work it out themselves. Don't punk out now, he told himself.

The Sigurdssons wanted Mischief Point. They wanted Snorri's camp. And they wanted Snorri Hallgrimsson somewhere the Manitoba Court of Appeal didn't ever hear from.

Snorri turned his boat in and hugged the shore as best he could, maybe twenty feet from the edge. They had shelter from the worst wind and waves but Snorri was tense.

"Rocks under the water. Nothing marked. I have to remember."

Snorri had to fight the waves now and Cal thought they were in danger of having their heads cracked open on the rocks just below the surface or on shore. Snorri took them through an obstacle course only he could see.

"Almost."

"Almost what?" said Cal.

Snorri pointed to a modest jut of land. A few lonely and wind-pruned trees stood guard on its point, above the smooth rock and dry, brittle moss. The trees grew thick further inland. The currents were tricky. Swells jostled and fought for sway. It was a bay with some protection from the wind but Cal couldn't believe Snorri would fish here.

"You put your nets in here?"

"This isn't the bay. Across!" He motioned.

Water spun the boat. A wave came over the back and the motor coughed and sputtered. Snorri cursed and threw himself at it, checked it. He rushed back to steer, the motor with two cylinders gone. Slow and sluggish, the boat turned to climb a swell. It tipped one way, then another. Cal saw water at his ankles. He grabbed the oar and tipped its blade over the side, not sure how he could possibly help.

A wave approached. Both Cal and Snorri saw it coming. It slammed into them and pushed them towards shore. The boat got up over some of the wave and climbed. Kept climbing. It dropped with a thud at the foot of the next wave. Water crashed into the boat. With a sickening jolt Cal felt the hull angle down. He lost his footing.

He saw Snorri off his feet, clutching his steering wheel with one hand. They were within a few feet of shore. Snorri rushed to the motor and pulled it up to save the propeller, then sank back down.

He and Cal just stared at each other a moment. Then

laughed.

"Well, that was something, Snorri."

"Yah."

They pulled themselves up. "This tree there," said Snorri. He pushed the boat out a little with the oar, dropped the motor again, and slowly eased forward. They were nearly touching it when Cal saw it. An opening. Snorri threaded the boat through a channel barely wide enough for it. Cal looked about at the dense forest on either side. Two or three minutes later the channel opened. Snorri cut the motor.

It was a haven. Water flat as glass. It looked as though no human may have entered the bay before. The smell of the forest, the sound of birds in the distance, the calm, undisturbed water, it was better than a shot of rye. Cal wanted to have nothing on him but a camera.

The boat coasted into the bay a little further, slowly stopped. They looked about them. Said nothing. Cal was unexpectedly moved. He let out a long breath. Thought of summers in his childhood. He stood up. Took it all in. "It's beautiful."

A loud crack reverberated through his skull. The bay spun into boat bottom and darkness filled his periphery. The back of his skull on fire, Cal tried to speak. His wide eyes couldn't focus. His limbs were useless. He felt hands grab his torso and he groaned. Then he was enveloped by cold, impossible cold. That shocked him to some semblance of alertness. He sputtered, and realized he was in the water. A few feet away from the boat. Snorri was standing, looking ready to move fast if need be, that inscrutable fishermen's smile on his face. He dropped the wrench held at his side. Cal reached back, touched the back of his head and winced. Hard to tell, but he guessed he was bleeding. Still his tongue wouldn't work in his mouth. His limbs no better. He was left bobbing in the water with, he was sure, a stupid look on his face.

Snorri disappeared down behind the rim of the boat. Away

from Cal's view he puttered with the lock on his lockbox, flipped open the lid and pulled out a rifle in its protective camouflage covering.

He appeared before Cal again, pulling the cover from his rifle. He checked it over carefully before slowly bringing it up to his shoulder and aiming down his sight.

"The fish's secret isn't the spot. It's the food."

Cal tried to move, to make a splash at least. The sound of a shot echoed off the still water.

For Love of Three Oranges

THE KING, THOUGH he was a good and powerful King, believed he would never find a Queen, so when at last he did find her she was sunlight to his skin, breath to his lungs. She was all alone in this world, and maybe that's what first caught his eye. Whatever it was, attention soon flowered into need. He shared of himself, and his entire kingdom, and wed her in an hour of when she said she would. He loved fully, if not wisely.

The Queen said little, but was full of joy, overflowing with warm embraces and pieces of strange songs, with no care for royal etiquette. Soon the whole kingdom came to love her. She behaved as though she could not see life's confinements, but somehow seemed no less confined.

It was the King's dream for a while, and the Queen bore two children, a boy and a girl. But she was weak after the boy's birth, very weak, and in the winter after that she took an ill turn, and died. Some said she was from the Land Beneath the Waves and she was too beautiful to be kept in this land for too long.

The King was inconsolable. After many days, he came out

from his dark quarters, for the sake of his children. But he issued his Royal Decree. On pain of death, instant, merciless death, there will be no more oranges in my kingdom, he said. Not one single sweet orb. Not one quarter, not one rind, not a single seed. Blood will spill on any soil where an orange dares to grow. And not an orange tree in all the land is to be left standing.

The Queen had enjoyed few pleasures more than eating oranges, and in fact the kingdom was known far and wide for the splendid quality of its oranges, but the King's will was carried out. There was extra wood for the hearths for a very short time, and soon there were no more oranges.

Slowly grief subsided. Not gone, but back beneath the daily chores and business of the living. Life in the land returned to how it was, perhaps just a little less sweet.

The King resumed the duties of his rule, but still doted on his children in their castle by the sea. He ached for his children's loss of a mother, so fine a mother, and especially for his son, who he feared was too young to even remember she existed. Always aware of their loss, he sought to make up for it, turning all his kingly powers to their safety, their comfort, and their happiness.

Afternoons were for petitions, reports and decrees, but the first few hours of every day were spent with his children in a simple kitchen in a tower, attached to the palace walls, looking down on the sandy shore. The King made their breakfasts with not one servant in sight. He would start the fire himself, and set the placings, and make the stacks of pancakes and pile them on plates. The Princessa buttered and cut her little brother's pancakes, and only she could do it exactly right.

Then one morning the garden gate creaked in the breeze, open.

The King noticed it from his kitchen window. He called for his son. Went into the yard. The Princessa, hearing something unfamiliar in her father's voice, followed him. Her brother had been nearby a moment ago.

They walked out the gate. Did the precocious child learn to open it for the first time? Did the King carelessly leave it open? A servant? Calling the boy's name, louder now, the King ran down to the beach. The Princessa raced after him. The King cast his gaze about, left and right, and saw fresh tracks in the sand. His pace quickened. The tracks turned into distinct little footprints where the dry sand turned to wet. They went to the water's edge. Tossing forwards and backwards in the surf was one tiny shoe.

"No…" whispered the King.

The King and the Princessa looked out at the crashing waves. The King knew his little boy was there, not far, just beneath the water somewhere, and at that moment and for a few moments more still alive, choking, clawing at blackness, afraid, uncomprehending. Close enough to be heard crying for his mother or father if his mouth wasn't full of water.

The King fell to his knees, clutched his daughter's hand so hard it nearly snapped, but the Princessa seemed not to notice and seemed not to understand. She stared at the shifting spaces between the waves.

The King would have stayed there, on his knees, at the water, till nightfall, till another nightfall after that, but eventually he realized his daughter was still at his side, so he took her up in his arms and carried her inside.

The Princessa's little brother was lost to them. From smiling in the kitchen to gone forever in less time than it takes a kettle to boil. He would never learn the alphabet, never play an instrument, never climb a tree, never explore the land, never break a bone, never tell a tale or joke or lie, never grow up. Never see or taste an orange.

The body never washed ashore. The casket contained one shoe, a toy wooden horse, a favourite blanket and a letter tied with a ribbon. After the funeral the King installed the Princessa in a castle keep surrounded by gardens and trees but far from the tall outer palace walls. Its only entrance, a heavy oak door, was kept locked and guards were placed around it and throughout the keep day and night. It was protected by the wits of the King's generals, and by other less obvious ways. The Princessa was never allowed out. She had tutors from all across the land, and jesters and singers and acrobats, and even a few friends her own age, from among the nobility, who were permitted to visit on occasion. But it was not the life the Princessa wanted. She grew taller, and fairer, and lonelier as she neared the end of her childhood days.

The days passed, then one warm and pleasant day a boy was wandering the palace grounds, which he was not allowed to do, and chanced to look up at an open window and spy the Princessa. He was struck. For several moments he just watched her. She had her eye to a looking-glass, looking far away. The Boy stood very still. Like a child, he did not want the moment to end.

"I can see you down there," she said.

"I know."

"Is there something you wish to say?"

"No. Yes. Do you live here?"

"I do."

"I live in the village. Are you the Princessa?"

"I am."

"You're not what I expected."

"What did you expect?"

"Someone selfish. Unkind."

"Maybe I am those things."

"No, I don't think so."

"Well, thank you."

"You look very lonely up there."

"What does lonely look like from down there?"

"Well, you're by yourself. Except for your looking-glass. Why don't you come down and walk with me?"

"I can't leave these quarters."

"I won't tell."

"You don't understand. I'm a prisoner here. I can't leave."

"Jump down and I'll catch you."

Almost a laugh. "I believe you would. But I can't throw myself and I can't be caught."

"I don't understand."

"It's a curse of my father's. He doesn't mean it to be a curse, of course. But…"

"Your father? So you didn't step on a witch, or steal her treasure, or refuse to marry someone?"

"No."

"Do you ever leave here?"

"No."

"It's not right. You should run away with me."

"Where?"

"Far away."

"How?"

"There must be a way."

"You would set me free?"

"Tell me how."

"You must fall in love with three oranges."

The Boy stared up as though an explanation might drop down from the sky, but none did. "…What?"

The sound of a snapping twig reached their ears.

"You must go! Quickly! It's not safe!"

"I will do whatever it takes."

"Please go!"

Only because she disappeared from her window did he speed away before he could be discovered. He headed towards the main gate of the outer wall. On his way out he paused in the shadows of the palace garden, where it was darkest and overgrown. Though the sun was still high, under these trees the shadows were charcoal and India Ink. The Boy felt himself being watched.

"Who's there?"

"She is forbidden to you."

A tall, thin man, strangely but richly dressed, emerged from the trees.

"Who are you?" said the Boy.

"My name is Sileno."

"Your parents named you that?"

"No."

The Boy glanced left and right as though an explanation might appear around the stranger's shoulder, but none did. "…okay."

"I have been many things, to many masters. Of late I am advisor to the King."

"The King?"

"Don't look so frightened, boy. I'm not going to put you in a box and carry you away," said Sileno. He seemed to stay bent forward slightly, as though about to tell a little secret. "Above all things, I serve the Princessa. She is a wonderful creature."

"I love her."

"Love?" He said it like a reprimand. "Don't you know anything of love? Love will eat your heart like an apple. I would talk about it a little more carefully."

"Love is not careful."

"No, it is not." He sighed. "So you would break the spell?"

"Yes."

"I can start you on your path. But be warned. The way is… not safe." The thought of the Frog Prince, the Ogre and the Alchemist troubled him.

"I will do what needs to be done," said the Boy. He was nearly but not quite grown, and had not learned to doubt himself.

"You may, you may. The secret, my young friend, is oranges."

"Oranges?"

"To break the spell that holds her in the castle you must love three oranges."

"I don't understand."

"Not easy to achieve, certainly. But you have your goal. You have your task. Or three. What could be simpler?"

"I must love three oranges?"

"Yes, yes. Three oranges. Really, in life you won't find more clarity than this."

"But there aren't any oranges."

"No! There are three oranges scattered about this land. Just three. Not easy to get."

"So I must find them?"

"The first orange is in the throne room of the Frog Prince. Find the Frog Prince and find the orange."

"Then I'll leave today." The Boy turned to go.

"One last bit of advice. Once you leave the village, I would accept the first offer of help you receive," said Sileno. He added, "And I would decline the next offer after that," but the Boy was already walking away, busy with thoughts of tasks, and may not have heard.

The flower girl sold the day's flowers from the shade on the roadside. In the mornings she tended to her tomatoes and zucchinis, and picked her flowers from the woods, or in the fall picked mushrooms. In the afternoons she sold her flowers. By the next day what she hadn't sold would be wilted and dead from the heat. These she scattered with good cheer about her hovel.

Suddenly she noticed a figure nearby, sharing the shade. He must have come from the woods, not the road.

"It's you," she said.

"It is as I said. The boy leaves."

"What? When?"

"This very day. Perhaps an hour or two."

"Just like that?"

"He is in love."

She flinched and turned away from Sileno. Forced herself to look back directly into his eyes. "Why should I go? I'm fine here."

"He will not succeed without you."

"I don't want him to succeed."

"Without you, he will not return."

He bought a flower, tucked it through a buttonhole in his coat, and walked up the road. She pursed her lips at the circumstances before her and set forward.

The Boy took one last look at his village and the King's palace towering over it, put his loose sack of meagre possessions over his shoulder, and turned to the road. Soon he was round a bend and it was all out of sight.

Before he realized she was there, the girl who sold flowers was walking next to him. She had fresh flowers tucked behind her ears and a green branch turned into a walking stick, which seemed to him a good idea.

"So, it's true? You're leaving?" she said.

"Yes."

"For how long?"

"I don't know."

"Is it some adventure?"

"Better for me not to say."

"I'm leaving too. See?" She held up her small sack of things.

"Why?"

"Better for me not to say."

The Boy smiled and shrugged.

"Why don't we travel together? Two is better than one. Twice as good, I say. I can help you do whatever it is you're going to do."

The Boy was about to send her home when he remembered Sileno's advice. A strange one, but he knows a thing or two, thought the Boy. Knows more than a penniless boy who has never spent a night away from his village, anyway.

"You may not be able to help me. But fine. We can travel together."

They entered a dark forest, and that night slept in a clearing under countless stars.

They walked for several days, meeting with very few people, but the Boy asked whomever they did meet for word of the Frog Prince. But no one had ever heard of him.

Eventually they passed an inn at a crossroads, one neither of them knew of, and they knew they were far from home. Another day or two of lonely travel after that and they met a peddler on the road who had heard tales of the Frog Prince, but none he could remember just now. The next day they met a hunter and they traded fresh berries, which they'd spent two hours picking, for a scrawny rabbit. In the evening they discovered it was no bargain. The meat was rotten. But the hunter told them he had heard of the Frog Prince, and he was no one they would want to meet.

The Boy and the Girl came to a place where the woods thinned out, and some of the land was plowed, and to their relief travelers were not so rare. They met farmers going to market, and many of them had knowledge of the Frog Prince. He lived in a deep, dark cave somewhere on the other side of the hill. Others said he lived in a lake. One farmer had a cousin who swore that he had seen him once, skulking around someone's fields during a full moon. No one was impressed when they realized the two were actually looking for him. 'Why are you going there?' or 'He's best left to himself' ended the conversations.

As the sun settled down into the treetops the Boy and the Girl saw an old woman running around and around her crooked shack. The Boy asked her what was the matter.

"Can't you see? Are you blind? My rooster. He's escaped!"

The Boy, seeing she was in distress, chased after the rooster, jumping through bushes and under branches until the Girl was nearly doubled over with laughter and even the Old Woman had to snicker. Eventually the Boy struggled out of a thick bush beaming with pride and the rooster hanging upside down in his hand.

Grateful, the Old Woman invited them in to dinner, which was very unfortunate for the rooster but very satisfying for them. Of course around the embers of the cooking fire the talk turned to the Frog Prince.

"He lives just over the hill, nearby the next village, in a deep, dark hole in the ground," said the Old Woman. "There is an old fig tree visible from the path. Close by to that is the entrance to the Frog Prince's lair. You had best be careful though."

They thanked the Old Woman, and spent the night outside her shack, since three could not lie down inside it. In the morning they bid goodbye and set out. By afternoon they had found the fig tree and the dark pit. It had rough steps around its edges, but was not inviting. The Girl pursed her lips at the chasm and led them downwards, spiraling further and further into its dark depths. They came to the bottom and found a passageway. It was difficult to see, but all around them they could hear the echoing sound of frogs.

The passage widened into a small cave. Above somewhere there was an opening, because some light fell down around a figure before them. He sat in water no deeper than their ankles, his back to them, hunched over, his legs bent. His shoulders shook very gently as though he might be sobbing. But there was no sound from him. Just the frogs.

They moved into the cave, their feet splashing in the water.

The Frog Prince froze. "Who's there?"

"Just two wandering travelers," said the Boy.

"We don't mean to disturb you," said the Girl.

The Frog Prince wiped at his cheeks with his hand and turned around. "What are you doing here?"

"Come to see you."

"Visitors?" He came closer.

His skin was pale. He slouched and his eyes bulged to a distracting degree, a trait accentuated when he slowly blinked, which was often.

And now that their eyes adjusted a little to the light, they could see there were frogs everywhere, on his shoulders, in the pockets of the rags that passed for his clothes, on the walls, all around them in the water.

The Frog Prince eyed them both, but the Girl just a little bit longer. For a long moment no one said anything. Finally, the Boy spoke.

"Lots of frogs."

"Yes," said the Frog Prince.

"Do you eat them?" said the Girl.

The Frog Prince glared. "I wouldn't eat them," he said in a sulking tone.

"Well, it's a nice home," she said.

"I guess."

"No one to bother you down here."

"Not usually."

"Um, have you lived here long?" said the Boy.

"I lose track of time."

"Why do they call you the Frog Prince?" said the Girl.

"Because of the frogs, I guess."

"It's mean."

"Well, it feels mean."

"I wonder if...?" said the Boy. If he was expecting the Frog Prince to politely enquire after him, he was mistaken. He came to the point. "Do you have an orange down here?"

"What is it to you?" The Frog Prince took a step back.

"We mean you no trouble. You can see we're not the King's soldiers."

"Why do you ask about an orange?"

"I wouldn't ask, but it's very important."

"How important?"

"It will bring my love to me."

"The orange is very precious to me. I have nothing else like it down here."

"Give me your terms. But I must have it."

"Will you bargain for it? Trade anything you have for the orange?"

The Boy, not having very much, readily agreed. The Frog Prince stared at him a moment, then turned away.

"Come then. This way, this way," he called after them. He led them to a dark corner, which turned into another passage, narrower than the first. After a few turns they came to another room much like the first. It too had water up to the ankles, and an opening far above that shone light on the center of the cave, only here there was a narrow rock in the center, about chest high and flat on the top. On the center of that sat a large and plump orange.

"I call this my throne room," said the Frog Prince.

"Look at it," said the Girl. She had not seen an orange in a very long time, and this seemed to be one of the finest oranges you could imagine.

"When the orange is gone you can sit in its place," said the Frog Prince.

"What?" said the Girl.

"Not really. You can sit wherever you like. Anywhere you choose."

"What are you talking about?" said the Boy.

"The orange for the girl. That's the bargain."

Realization dawned on the Boy but not quickly. "I'm not

trading a person."

"You made a bargain."

The Boy looked at the Frog Prince, expecting him to break into a smile, but he didn't. "She's not staying here with you."

"No orange for you then."

"You can have anything in my bag. Or anything else I can get you."

"I want her!"

"Well you can't have her."

"Not fair! Not fair!"

The Frog Prince charged at the Boy. Together they skidded across the muddy cave floor. The Frog Prince pulled at the Boy's hair. The Boy elbowed him in the cheek. They wrestled to get on top of each other.

"Stop it, both of you!" said the Girl.

They both got to their feet, holding onto and shoving each other.

"Just stop it!"

The Boy punched the Frog Prince in the belly. The Frog Prince pulled on the Boy's ears as hard as he could. The Boy shoved against him.

The Frog Prince's foot slipped in the muck and the Boy threw him hard against the wall. Then the Boy landed a vicious kick. Then two more. The Frog Prince curled into a ball and whimpered. The Boy picked up his bag, now sopping wet he noticed with bad temper, and retrieved a piece of rope. He proceeded to tie the Frog Prince's legs tightly together. The Frog Prince grunted and moaned and tried to pull his legs away, but it was no use.

As the Boy finished the last of many knots he said, "See? I'm leaving the hands. Just your legs. You'll be able to get yourself loose."

The Girl, moved to pity by the sight of the muddy, defeated Frog Prince, apologized and kissed him on the forehead, but it enraged him.

"I'm not a child!"

"I'm sorry," she said.

"Then stay with me. I would treat you like a princess."

"I…"

"I know you won't."

"I don't think staying in this cave is good for you," said the Boy.

"Does he say things?" said the Frog Prince to the Girl. "Does he touch you? Do you want him to?"

"Enough," said the Boy.

"I can see how it is. You're a strong boy who can tie up other boys. I'm sure the girls have always liked you."

"I wish it didn't have to be this way, but I need that orange."

The Boy stood up, turned his attention to the orange, and took a few steps towards it. He hesitated, looked back at the Frog Prince on the ground.

"Go ahead. Take it," said the Frog Prince.

"Is it poison?"

"You say it will bring you love?"

"Yes."

"Then it's poison."

The Boy picked up the orange, admired it in his hand a moment, then tucked it deep down in his bag.

"Now go. Leave me alone," said the Frog Prince.

They readied to go. The Girl paused as if to say something, thought better of it, and soon the two of them were gone.

The Frog Prince made no effort to stand up or undo his knots.

"I will leave this cave someday and everyone will be sorry. You'll all know how it feels."

A small frog jumped up on the Frog Prince's shoulder. He scooped it up and squeezed it in his fist until it exploded in his hand.

"They'll all be sorry."

"Do you have it? Do you have the orange?" Sileno, who appeared unannounced, leaned in close so he could be seen by the firelight. The Boy was so startled he nearly jumped to his feet. He settled back down and reached into his bag.

"Yes, I have it."

"Don't take it out! Keep it put away. You have done well. Both of you."

"Thank you," said the Boy.

"But now is no time to dwell on past success. The next orange won't fall into your lap. The tasks become more difficult. You will have to be careful."

"I'm ready," said the Boy.

"So am I," said the Girl.

Sileno looked at their campsite. "You must be hungry."

"You have food?" said the Girl.

"No."

"Where do we go now? Is it far?" said the Boy.

"It is many days from here. Head towards where the sun sets. Eventually you will come to a forest that is darker and quieter than any you've been in before. Deep in this forest is a meadow. In this meadow is a cottage. The cottage is where the Ogre lives. The Ogre has the second orange."

"So we just wander as best we can deep into the forest?" said the Boy.

"Yes."

"No more directions than that?"

"No."

"How will we know we've found it?" said the Girl.

"If you find anything you'll know you're there. His is the only home in those parts."

Without a goodbye or any other word Sileno disappeared into the night.

Two servants lingered at a crossroads in the dying light.

"Bad luck to wait at a crossroads," said the taller of the two. "If he's not here before dark I won't stay."

"Fine. Go home then and tell the King you won't wait at crossroads," said the shorter one.

"Bad luck." The Tall Servant kicked at loose stones along the ground. "Do you have the bottle?"

"Saving it," said the Short Servant.

"What did I do to end up out here with no one but you for company?"

As the sun slipped below the tops of the trees the Tall Servant muttered to himself. He paced as the Short Servant sat and whittled a stick with an ugly looking blade. He tucked the blade away and threw away the stick when he noticed a figure approaching them at a leisurely pace.

"Is that him?" said the Tall Servant.

"Most likely."

"No hurry, is he? Strolling like a groomsman coming up the aisle."

At last he arrived in front of them. "I see fate has brought us together."

"Sir?" said the Short Servant.

"We was told to be here," said the Tall Servant.

"You grow old and die, so you see the will of men and women. If you went from grave to womb, you would see the fate," said Sileno.

"It's bad luck to speak of fate at a crossroads. You might invite strange folk," said the Tall Servant.

"Maybe I am strange?"

"In that case I want three wishes."

"Such as?"

"I want riches. And women. All the women I've ever wanted. And I want to be young forever."

"I could give you a little of all those things. But you wouldn't be satisfied."

"Pay him no mind, Sir," said the Short Servant, not liking where this was going.

"You should want less. All suffering in this world comes from want."

"Even so, we want to get to things. And get home," said the Tall Servant.

"If you please," said the Short Servant.

"The boy. The one who travels with that girl," said Sileno.

"The one sells flowers?" said the Short Servant.

"That's her. The two of them are up to something."

"Up to no good?" said the Tall Servant.

"It doesn't matter. All that matters is the King doesn't want it done. Can he rely on you?"

"He can," said the Short Servant. "We know there was some foolishness before. But that's past."

"We're glad to be of use."

"Has it been explained to you?" said Sileno.

"It has."

"You must stop the boy from completing his tasks. The safety of the Princessa depends on you."

"The Princessa?" said the Tall Servant.

"Yes. The Princessa, who is worth more than gold. For whom the King will do anything to keep safe. Are you the men to do the job?"

"We are your men. Say the word and it will be done," said the Short Servant.

"It's the King's word, not mine."

"We will stop the boy," said the Tall Servant.

"Whatever it takes," said the Tall Servant.

"They passed this way not so long ago. That way." Sileno pointed. "They are a day or two ahead of you, at most."

"Then we are on our way," said the Short Servant.

The Boy and the Girl followed the setting sun, and as Sileno had promised the woods slowly became as dark and as quiet as any they could imagine. They did not meet anyone. Neither did they see or hear any animals. Further on the birds fell silent. After that they realized even the wind and the trees gave no sound. The forest over their heads grew so thick they began to miss the sky. There ceased to be any path, at least any path made by men. At times they followed what may have been animal trails, though what animal they couldn't say. Still they pushed on between trees, through branches, over clearings.

Then it was there. A tidy cottage. Around it was a large garden overflowing with vegetables. To one side there were rows of vine tomatoes on trellises as high as their heads. Under the cottage windows were beds of dark red carnations. The back of the cottage disappeared into a hill. Just outside was an old man with a water bucket.

"Hello," said the Girl.

"Hello," said the old man.

"It's a beautiful garden."

"Why, thank you. It's a good year."

"I imagine it fills your plate."

"And my cup. I grow some marvelous teas. What brings you to this part of the forest?"

"I'm looking for an orange," said the Boy.

"An orange?"

"Yes."

"You must have traveled a long way."

"Why do you say that?" said the Boy.

"Because you're here. This is a long way from anywhere."

"Oh. Well, we have traveled far."

"Poor souls. So far away from all those who know and care for you. So brave. You wouldn't catch me out there somewhere, away from my comforts. But why so much trouble for an orange? There are other fruits."

They had no answer.

"Well, you may as well come in. I have biscuits."

He led them into his front room, which was a kitchen and sitting room together in one. The room and its furnishings were humble and simple, but tidy and clean.

"You must have some tea," said the old man. "Please, make yourselves at home. Rest yourselves. Put down your bags. Where is that tea pot?"

"Don't go to any trouble. You can pour into our mugs straight from the kettle," said the Boy.

"Don't be silly. I have a tea pot for company. From the kettle." He shook his head. "Ah, here it is." He set the tea pot on the table and put the kettle on his little stove, then put another log in the stove and set about starting his fire again from the glowing embers. "That shouldn't be too long."

He went to his cupboard for tea. "I'm known for my tea. The first bit of warm water I swish around the pot and throw out. You must warm the pot. You must never put hot tea in a cold pot. Puts the tea off."

"Really?" said the Boy.

"Oh, yes."

The Girl and the Boy looked at each other. The Boy shrugged.

"They call you the Ogre?" asked the Girl, which made the Boy start.

He nodded. "They do, they do. Someone's little joke, I suppose."

When the kettle let out its shrill whistle the Ogre rushed to take it off the stove before it got too hot. He put one then two splashes of water into his tea pot, swished the water around for a moment, then threw the water outside his front door. Then he put his tea in the pot and carefully poured. He set the tea pot and three cups, chipped but once of fine quality, down on the table. Lastly he put out a plate of very stale biscuits.

"Help yourself. Don't be shy."

They did, though the Boy didn't touch the biscuits, which he thought could be older than he was.

"Mmm. It's very good," said the Girl.

"Chamomile. And I've added gooseberries," said the Ogre. "Is your stomach upset?" he asked the Boy.

"Just not hungry, thanks," which was not true.

They sipped their tea and exchanged pleasantries about the weather. The Ogre described at length the local soil conditions. Deciding their interest, after a time, was lagging, he changed the subject.

"So, you said you were looking for an orange?"

The Boy sat up a little straighter. "Yes."

"A strange thing to be wandering these woods for, I have to say."

"Do you have an orange?"

"Well, I just might. I have many odds and ends and curiosities around my little place, most of them gathering dust. And an orange. I don't have much use for that. My tastes don't run to oranges." The Ogre poured more tea in each of their cups, his own last. "But do you know, now that I think on it, I believe I do have an orange around here somewhere. I'd have to look. But what do you need it so badly for?"

The Boy blushed.

The Ogre understood. "Ah. Love. It makes us sick, and it makes us well. Could have made me well, anyway. No wonder your stomach is upset."

"Would you be willing to part with it?" said the Boy.

"Well, I don't know. I tell you what. You want it? You'll have to beat me at my rope game."

"What's that?"

"Just a little game of mine. Have you never played?"

"No."

"It's not difficult to learn. I tie up your hands and you try to get them free. If you do, then you tie up my hands and I try to get free. Who ever does the best knots wins."

"And if I lose?" said the Boy, thinking of the Frog Prince.

"Then you get no orange. That's all. If you like you can fetch me some more water from the spring. But I'll warn you, I'm very good at knots."

"All right. Let's play."

The Ogre took a rope out of a drawer. He showed the Boy how to put his wrists together, then he wrapped the rope around them, tying a series of knots with practiced ease.

"Maybe we should play something else," said the Girl, but the Ogre shushed her.

The Ogre finished by pulling the knots tight with more power than he seemed capable of. "There."

The Boy tried to pull and twist his hands a little apart. "It's tight," he said. He struggled to free himself. "I can't get loose." He tried to loosen the knots with his teeth but it got him nowhere. His hands began to turn numb and also pale. "It's too tight."

"Do you give up already?" The Ogre watched all his toiling with a little smile.

The Boy thought of the orange and the Princessa. For several more moments he struggled with all his might. He was angry with himself, but could see it was no use. "I can't do it."

The Boy's hands were now a sickly pale. "Untie him," said the Girl.

"Not yet."

"Get it off!" said the Boy. Desperate, he tried to scrape the rope from his wrists with the edge of the table.

"Untie him!"

"Don't you bark at me! Everything in my cottage happens exactly as I say."

With a sudden burst of movement the Ogre grabbed up a log by the stove and knocked the Boy to the floor. He lay still. The Girl screamed. The Ogre raised the log high and brought it down again on the Boy's head. He dropped the bloody log and went to the drawer. He pulled out another piece of rope.

"Give me your hands."

"I will not!" She backed away.

"It's my game! Not yours!" The Ogre let out a scream of his own and grabbed at her wrist. She was amazed at his strength, but in her panic she twisted away and threw off his grip as she would have if a python had sunk its fangs in her wrist. She ran through the closest door, deeper into the house.

The first room she ran into was spare and plain. There were no windows and no furniture except a single table. At its centre was a plate with a polished orange sitting on it. Seeing nowhere to hide, and much preferring running to hiding, the Girl ran into the next room.

The second room was nearly full to the ceiling with piles of travelers' sacks stacked high. Some of the sacks looked very old. A few had belongings pulled out of them, but most seemed untouched.

"You're a little cheater," called the Ogre from the first room.

The Girl ran into a third room. It had windows, but she pulled back the drapes to see they were far too small for her to crawl through. Behind her, in the sunlight, were several jars scattered about tables and shelves. She stared, confused, then thought of the village butcher, and realized with a shiver that there were livers and kidneys floating in the jars.

"Where are you, my little mouse?"

She ran on. The next room was pitch dark and that scared her even more than the last, but running forward she found a wall and followed that until she felt a door, then its handle, and she tumbled into a long, narrow hallway.

"You can't hide from me, little mouse."

The Girl turned to see the Ogre at the other end of the hall. She ran through the nearest door and locked it behind her. Soon there was a furious pounding and she thought it must soon break.

The room appeared to be a dining room. There was nothing unusual about it, but she shuddered to think what was served there.

This room had one other door than the one she had come in by. She went through it, closed it behind her, and was in a very small room. It had another door and she saw lying close to it a pair of boots. Filled with hope she threw it open and found herself outside, looking at rows of tomatoes.

There was a loud crash behind her. She hid in the tomatoes.

Soon the Ogre was at his back door. "You've found a different maze, little mouse? There's no one to save you."

He called out for her. She darted in and out of the rows. She crouched as low as she could without slowing down. The Ogre moved up and down the rows much more swiftly than he seemed capable of, occasionally holding his eye up to the trellis, heavy with vines, and trying to spot her.

"I will find you."

Creeping backwards from his voice, she stepped on a hand rake. She picked it up without a thought. Hearing his voice come closer, she ran again, changing rows often, but always with terror, afraid she would pop straight into his view.

"I can hear your breath," said the Ogre, and he chuckled.

Then he thrust his head through the trellis, among the tomatoes, right in front of her.

The Girl plunged the hand fork into the Ogre's neck, just under his chin. She pulled away, and the fork stayed in his neck, until he pawed at it and it fell to the ground.

The Ogre dropped down to all fours. He crawled towards the Girl, trying to keep one hand on his throat, as she retreated down the row. The row came to a dead end. Though it wouldn't have been hard to push her way through she fell to her knees and wrapped her arms around herself.

The Ogre crawled closer and closer. Blood ran down from

his neck, over his hand and through his fingers, into the ground, turning dark soil black. He now produced a steady gurgling sound.

The Girl curled into a ball and began to shake. She tightened her eyes shut.

The Ogre crawled closer. He went down on his belly, but staring at her with pure hatred, he pulled himself forward on his elbows. She could hear the gurgling sound get louder and louder, closer and closer.

The Ogre reached for her, his arm outstretched, and grabbed a fistful of dirt just in front of her. His head went down. His fist stayed tight but his whole body went still. There was no sound.

After a long moment of silence the Girl opened her eyes. The soil around the Ogre was damp and black, and left her hands red when she pushed herself to her feet.

Sobbing, she ran around the cottage and in the front door. The Boy hadn't moved. She tried to wake him, slapped his cheeks too gently to do anything, then rummaged through the drawers. She found a knife, rusty and stained and dirty with what she did not want to think about. She carefully cut away at the rope, with its clever knots, and set his hands free.

The Boy came to his senses, and rubbed his hands together, trying to get the blood back into them.

She found a cloth for him to hold to his head. Then, still trying to control her sobs, she dragged the Boy outside, and when she calmed down enough she told him what had happened.

"I owe you my life," he said.

"You would do the same," she said.

The Boy had her show him where the Ogre lay. He wanted to be sure they were safe. That the Ogre wasn't hiding in the woods waiting to pounce again. But the Ogre remained exactly as he was. Not knowing exactly what else to do, they dug a shallow grave as best they could with yard tools and buried him in the garden. Then the Boy went inside a moment and returned with the orange, and their bags. They filled them with vegetables from the garden and returned back the way they had come.

After some days, they came out of the dark and quiet forest, though they were far from certain of where they were. They hoped it was more or less the place they had set out from after their last meeting with Sileno. They were unsure what to do next if he did not present himself, but they need not have worried. They soon found Sileno standing by a stream, fishing.

"Sileno?"

"Shh. I think I have a bite."

"We have the orange," said the Boy.

"Most impressive. Just a moment." He yanked on his fishing pole and lifted it into the air. There was no fish on the line. He sighed.

"We almost died," said the Boy.

"I warned you it was dangerous. But I'm relieved to see it went well."

"It did not go well," said the Girl.

He looked at her closely. "No, I can see by your face it did not. For that I am sorry. But you are alive. And you have the orange. Wait." He stared at his line. Waved his fishing pole slowly back and forth over the stream. "Never mind. Just the current."

"What now?" said the Boy.

"It takes patience. You've made yourself ready. Now you wait for the moment. A certain stillness is required. Then, if fate favours you, the current brings you a fish that's tempted by your bait and you pull it in."

"I mean for us."

"Ah, yes. Well, you – Aha!" The line jerked. The fishing pole bent and Sileno yanked it one way then another. "I have it!" He raised the pole higher and a fish splashed on the surface. "Have you heard of the Cave of the Sacred Heart?"

"No."

He pulled the fish from the water. It thrashed about. Sileno got one hand on it, dropped his pole and proceeded to remove the hook from its mouth.

"Easy, little fish. Don't feel so bad. Some day a very large fish will swallow up me. Metaphorically, I suspect. But one never knows."

The fish tried to wriggle out of his hand. Sileno turned his attention back to the Boy and the Girl.

"You must go to the Cave of the Sacred Heart. There you will find the Alchemist. He has the third and final orange. But be careful."

"He can't be worse than the Ogre," said the Boy.

"He is worse," said Sileno, with an edge in his voice. He softened his tone. "Make no mistake, you are in a very serious business." He slammed the fish against a sharp rock on the stream's bank. It stopped moving. "Nothing precious in this world is cheaply earned. And what you seek is precious. There is a road just over there. Follow it until it takes you to the Cave of the Sacred Heart."

"What then?"

"When you have the third orange make your way back towards this spot. I will find you somewhere along the road. I will be watching for you."

As Sileno left he threw the fish to them. That evening they cooked it, along with vegetables from the Ogre's garden, and it seemed such a sumptuous feast that they could not help but laugh and tell stories to each other, despite the difficult days.

The Princessa stared out her window as the sun set. Soon it would pass beneath the outer wall where it would continue skipping its reflected light across the surface of the ocean, far away from her, leaving her in gloom.

Sileno appeared behind her. She did not turn, did not see him, but knew he was now there. For a little while they said nothing, watching the sunset together.

"They say my father did not love wisely."

"Love is many things, but not wise."

Sileno came into the centre of the room and placed a large, ripe tomato in a bowl on the table. "The Ogre is dead. The boy has the second orange."

"The way he looked at me. Does he really love me?"

"Who can say?"

"Tell me the truth."

"He loves you."

"He would do anything for me?"

"Yes."

"And I will break his heart."

"You can't help what you feel, Princessa. You can't help what you are."

"And what am I?"

"You are a creature that was never meant to be caged. Just like your mother." Sileno put a hand on her shoulder. "You do not ask for too much, Princessa. The spell will be broken."

"My brother loved everything."

"I remember."

"Nothing can hurt him now?"

"No. Nothing."

"Does he still laugh and play?"

"The boy will succeed. He will open the way for you. You can leave this world, and join your mother and brother."

"I've missed them so much."

"You will see them again."

"You'll look after him, won't you? That poor, reckless boy? After I'm gone? Please say you will."

"...As you wish."

"And my father?"

"I will do whatever I can."

She turned back to the window as the last rays of sun lingered on her balcony.

"Poor father. What did a kingdom ever get you?"

It was a cooler than expected night but the two servants had a fire crackling by the side of the road that kept the chill away. In fact they had to open their coats a little. Their entire camp consisted of a bottle of Tempranillo, a small bottle of olive oil, and part of a wheel of Manchego, all within reach.

The Tall Servant held two slices of bread over the fire with a forked stick, toasting them with much care.

"Careful," said the Short Servant. "That's the last of it."

"I won't burn it. Now let's have a taste."

The Short Servant uncorked the Tempranillo, took a long swig, and passed it to the Tall Servant, who also drank deeply.

"A toast. To us," said the Short Servant, taking the bottle back. He drank and the Tall Servant grabbed the bottle and did the same.

"To us."

"Doing the King's work," said the Short Servant.

"We are brave."

"And loyal."

"Yes, loyal too. Fortune smiles on the brave and loyal."

"We'll be made generals."

"We will be important men," said the Tall Servant. He began to rub the toasted bread with garlic.

"Everyone will say so."

"I will buy my mother cows. Big, fat ones."

"Wait till the village sees. We will have banquets. With white napkins. And bowls of water just to wash your fingers in."

"And the food. More food than there are plates. Pass the olive oil."

The Short Servant passed him the bottle. The Tall Servant drizzled olive oil over the bread and let it soak in. They continued to take turns drinking the wine.

"One simple task and we're on our way," said the Tall Servant.

"But let's not look too far ahead. This stupid boy. If we're not careful he'll ruin everything. He dares to insult the King. What won't he do?"

"He thinks he can love whoever he wants?"

"Exactly. He's like a thief."

"And a traitor."

"Is someone like that going to listen to reason? No."

"Definitely not."

"We know what the fool will understand."

"Damn him."

"Right."

"It's ready," said the Tall Servant.

The Short Servant cut generous slabs of Manchego and placed them on the toast to melt. "Don't let it melt too much. I don't want any falling into the fire."

"When we get home we'll have all the cheese and bread we could want. And wine."

Soon they ate their toast and licked their fingers and thought of home.

The Boy and the Girl stayed to the road. It passed a large, important house, and they saw a young man toiling in its fields, pulling large rocks loose from the ground. The Boy thought the soil might yield more rocks than sprouting seeds. The young man kept looking over his shoulder, but paused long enough to describe to them the Cave of the Sacred Heart. They took their leave, and the young man quickened the pace of his efforts.

The Cave of the Sacred Heart was in the base of a small mountain that had several jagged peaks like crooked teeth. The Boy and the Girl trudged on. The woods became sparse, and the ground rockier. With less shelter above them the sun brought down a heat that felt as if it might push them into the dirt. The Boy felt like complaining but the Girl never did, and even now she had a fresh flower behind her ear, picked that morning, and her back was straight, so he said nothing. They rested longer wherever they found shade. They were hot and tired when at last they saw the place where the Alchemist lived.

The mountain was as it had been described, and they could easily pick it out from a distance. The cave was neither hard to find, nor obvious. They walked around the little mountain until they found the entrance's rough stone steps. There was nothing else to indicate its purpose.

It was not a very deep cave, so there was just enough light to see by. They stood before the shrine at the back of the cave. On the altar were drippings of candles left to burn until they were gone, and offerings of flowers, turned almost to dust, and wine stains. But it appeared that nothing on the altar had been left there recently.

"What now?" said the Girl.

The Boy studied the altar. Wandered in front of it. Then he leaned over it. "The cave goes a little further back. There's a space behind the altar."

"How do we get to it?"

"This way." The Boy climbed over the altar and disappeared. The Girl hesitated at the potential affront to God, glanced around, then followed.

They crawled along a narrow opening in the rock. Soon they could stand and came up to a heavy door. It had a massive iron pad lock, but the lock was not in place. The Boy opened the door. It was pitch black, but they could both feel a fresh breeze on their face.

"I've seen enough of caves," said the Girl.

But the Boy eased the door shut behind them and they moved forward. The passageway moved upwards and a few minutes later opened into a narrow crevice. Their eyes adjusted to the afternoon light again. There was a path, or so they thought, that climbed steeply. They took it.

The way was not easy and they were both covered in sweat when they reached the top. They emerged from the rocky crevice into a small valley, closed in on all sides by the jagged peaks. They realized the valley was on top of the mountain, hidden by the peaks. The path winded up a small hill, where there sat an ancient fortress.

It was falling apart in places, with at least a part of the roof collapsed, and the walls toppled into piles of rubble. They walked up to the fortress. It was from an age gone by, and they would have expected to find an army, or no one but ghosts, so they were somehow a little surprised to find a lone man outside the front door. He was picking up clothes that had been left to dry in the sun on some nearby rocks. He saw them and smiled.

"So, two pilgrims at my door. And just in time."

"Who are you? What is this place?" said the Boy.

"I am a simple alchemist, and this is my castle. What do you think? Oh, it's true it's seen better days. Could use a few fresh bricks here and there. But it's home."

"You're the Alchemist?"

"You flatter me. I am an alchemist, I don't know about 'the.' To what do I owe the pleasure of this company?"

"We were sent here."

"Really? By whom?"

"His name is Sileno."

"Sileno? I've never heard of him. I'll have to thank him. So, are you here for wisdom?"

"Should we be?" said the Girl.

"No one comes here for nothing. Often it's wisdom. Advice. 'Should I plant this crop or that? What should I do with my children?' Sometimes they come for good health. Or good fortune. Even bravery. Sometimes they come for love. Because of the name of the shrine, I think."

"It sounds like they ask for a lot," said the Girl.

"I do what I can. False modesty aside, I am unrivalled in the arts of alchemy. It is my calling. No one leaves here disappointed. Why don't you stay for lunch and think about what you want?"

"Why not?" said the Boy.

"Very sensible. Welcome."

The Girl stared at the Boy's back, incredulous. But then she pursed her lips at the circumstances before her and set forward.

They entered the castle.

"This is my laboratory," said the Alchemist.

The huge room was filled with tables and shelves, which were cluttered. There were several brick furnaces, each with bellows that reached nearly waist high. Above them were clear tubes with liquids in them. The tubes twisted and turned this way and that. Most of the liquids were black, with some pinkish or red and one or two yellows and browns. A few connected to each other and wound around a corner or behind some apparatus and out of sight.

The Girl spotted the orange on a shelf, crowded to the side by casks labeled salt, sulphur and vinegar. She nudged the Boy and nodded towards the shelf. She had to nudge him again before his attention fell on it. The Alchemist followed their gaze.

"What? Oh yes, the orange. Quite rare and in fine condition.

Some droplets of its juice are missing, taken with my syringe apparatus, but not much. I soon lost interest in the orange's properties."

"Do you not need it anymore?" said the Girl.

"We'll see, we'll see."

They moved further into the great room. Every available space was occupied with sealed glass vessels, clay casks, cooking pots, stone bowls, droppers, vials and spoons, or other objects they couldn't identify. Many of the flasks were connected with tubes.

"What is all this for?" said the Boy.

"Glad you should ask. I am trying to distill truth from the universe."

"It looks complicated."

"It is, to be honest, very difficult work. Please, don't touch anything. We can talk in my study upstairs."

There was a faint banging noise in the distance.

"What is that?" said the Boy.

"The wind. It gets into every nook and cranny up here."

They climbed up to the Alchemist's study. The Alchemist looked at his two chairs with disappointment.

"Could you be so kind as to bring a chair up from downstairs?" he asked the Boy. "My apologies. I'm afraid my back is a little sore from stooping over my delicate work."

The Boy was not sorry to have a closer look at the laboratory. He went downstairs and quickly found a chair. But instead of returning right away he wandered about the room, which he was not supposed to do. Once again he heard a thumping sound, thump, thump, thump, but he could not find out from which direction it came, so he gave up. Near the centre of the room, where the Alchemist had not taken them, he bumped into a table, setting the many vials and bottles on it wobbling. The Boy reached out to settle them and began to read their labels. Strength. Love. Jealousy. Anger. Sleep. Fear. Sadness. Joy.

He was not sure if he believed it, but thinking to later impress the Princessa, he slipped a vial labeled 'Strength' into his pocket.

Upstairs, the Girl looked about the Alchemist's study. There was a simple wooden table, with three small cups sitting on it, the two chairs, and shelves of old books along the walls. Behind the Alchemist was an arched window, without glass or shutters to keep out the high winds.

"I've been expecting you," said the Alchemist.

"It's a splendid view," said the Girl.

"Here." He pushed a cup towards her. "It's a love potion."

"What?"

"I can see how it is. Have him drink this at the table while he's looking at you. You will be the only one he loves."

She looked at it a long moment before speaking. "No. It wouldn't be real."

The Alchemist scoffed. "What's real? I can make anyone feel anything. I can make myself feel anything. Is it not real? Because it feels real." The Alchemist warmed to his topic. "What is love, real love? It is certain potions, naturally occurring in the body, moving in concert to produce an effect. You saw that boy and something moved about your bloodstream. Who can say why? But you felt it. Felt it more than anything.

"So what if this boy feels the liquid humors trigger love in his heart because of a potion he sipped? Is it really any better, or any more reasonable, to fall in love at a glimpse into the eyes or at a scrap of song? Some half-remembered stimulus in a weak moment? I think not."

"I don't believe you."

"Love makes life sweeter. But why do you think that is? Because potions in the blood say so to the brain. That's all it is. So let him drink."

"I can't do it."

"So be it. But don't say you never had a chance. When you watch him marry her, and imagine them on their wedding night, remember it didn't have to happen. You let it happen."

The Boy returned with the chair.

"Ah, thank you." The Alchemist took the chair and sat. "Please sit."

They did, and the Alchemist pushed the cup towards the Boy. "Please. You must be thirsty."

"What is it?"

"Something to lift your spirits a little."

The Boy looked at the Girl with some curiosity, but she said nothing. He lifted the cup, and then she tried to say 'wait' but the Boy knocked the drink back in one movement.

The Alchemist watched them both. "There's been a mistake. She meant to give you a love potion."

"What?"

"I didn't…"

"But it's a truth potion. Well, not something to waste." He turned to the Girl. "Ask him."

She understood what he meant. "No. Please."

"Do you love her?"

There was a pause, but not very long.

"No." The Boy saw he wounded her. Saw a tear in her eye. "The Princessa. I don't know, maybe it could have been different. But… no."

"A princessa? Very interesting." The Alchemist looked at the Girl closely, spoke almost in her ear, like an intimate friend. "You hurt. In pain."

"Yes."

He turned to the Boy. "And you, you feel guilt. Terrible guilt."

"Yes."

"That's how it is. Pain and guilt. But there is remedy. I can help." He slid the two remaining cups towards them. "Drink. Drink and you will feel content. Happy."

They slowly put their hands around their cups and raised them. The Boy peered in his and sniffed it. He thought of the

Girl, what he had put her through, and brought the cup to his lips and drank. Seeing him do so, the Girl did the same.

The Alchemist smiled, showing his teeth. "There has been a mistake."

"What?" said the Boy.

"A sleeping potion."

The Boy awoke with a start. He breathed in a rotting stench that made him retch onto himself. With horror he realized he was in a chamber exactly like a funnel, with sides of iron. It left him barely enough room to move around inside it. Sitting on top was a heavy lead lid with several air holes across it. It was so heavy and thick the Boy thought it must have taken five men to move it.

The gagging putrefaction caused a panic in him. He tried to move the lid but it wouldn't budge. He twisted around in the chamber, sliding his hands against the sides that were slick with black slime. He imagined he could feel maggots wriggling against his skin. His fingers felt bits of bone and scraps of cloth. And he knew by the cloth that it was not the rancid, disintegrated flesh and organs of forest animals that he sat in.

The Boy felt like he was falling, falling out of himself, but the dark iron prison wouldn't let him go. He thought about what other travelers may have been here before him, and the revulsion coursed through him with such force that he retched again. He wept a little to himself. Then he remembered the vial in his pocket. With shaking hands he pulled the stopper and poured the liquid down his throat. At first he felt nothing. Then a rush of warmth went through his belly. It spread to his arms and legs. It stoked his fear into anger. The Boy braced his body against the sides of his prison as best he could and pushed at the lid. To his great surprise and relief, it moved easily. He had to grab at it to keep it from clattering to the ground. He held it with one hand while he climbed down. He could see his funnel chamber fed into one of the many tubes he had seen.

He crept about the Alchemist's lair. He listened intently, but there was no knocking or bumping sound any longer. He followed the tubes over his head to their source, dozens of chambers like the one he had been trapped in. He looked at them a moment as though they might disappear if he wished hard enough. He climbed up to one and pried off its lid. Inside was a decomposing corpse, rotting flesh falling away on one side to reveal its skull. The Boy retched onto the floor down below.

The Boy saw the orange on its shelf, but he was desperate to free the Girl from her nightmarish circumstances and scarcely gave it a thought. However, he saw the table of potions again and went through them all, examining each label.

He moved to another chamber. Found nothing but bits of bone and slime inside. Then another. He began to move more quickly, scared for the Girl and fearing the worst. Another chamber held rotting remains of two people with limbs wrapped around each other. Lovers? Siblings? It filled him with disgust and rage that he would never know. Yet another held a shrunken corpse, or else a smaller victim. Quite small. The Boy gave up quietness, working more quickly and raising his whispers as loud as he dared, calling for her.

At last he flung a lead cover off a chamber and found her. She was staring up at him, wide-eyed. They embraced. "It's… it's…" She could say no more.

"I know."

She slipped and slid but he reached down and lifted her out. She wiped away at herself, but her hands were as filthy as the rest of her. Her whole body shook for several minutes before she could properly walk.

"We have to get out of here," said the Boy. She nodded. He took her by the shoulder and they looked for their escape.

The Boy and the Girl turned down an aisle and came face to face with the Alchemist. At the sight of the two of them loose in his lab he was deeply shocked, but he was also very proud and quickly recovered himself.

"How ever did you get out?" he said.

"We'll just take our leave, no thanks to you," said the Boy.

"What's wrong? You've seen how the sausage gets made?"

"You were going to let us rot alive!" said the Girl.

"Necessary for the process. Believe me, I don't enjoy it. Of course, I didn't start with this. Trials and tests led me up to it."

The Alchemist was all calm and confidence, but it was a fragile thing. Having two upset people in his laboratory was very troubling for him. He'd never had to deal much with visitors who weren't helpless, and he was very fussy about his work things.

"I'm very disappointed," said the Alchemist. "I would have united you two like no one else could. You would have made an exquisite sorrow potion."

"You're insane," said the Boy.

"I am older than I look. I have extended my youth beyond what most think possible, but soon I will discover immortal life!"

"I thought you were looking for truth?"

"They are different states of the same liquid."

"You're horrible. Just horrible," said the Girl.

"You lack understanding. You can't even conceive of the things I am achieving."

"A few potions of tricks. You could have used grapes instead of people and achieved much the same thing," said the Boy.

"You're a fool! I will be able to turn men into angels! We can make our own heaven."

"I've seen enough of your heaven," said the Girl.

"Open your eyes! You see how God made the world. You think he didn't do some terrible things?"

The Boy moved himself between the Alchemist and the Girl. "I'm going to put a stop to all of it."

"You?" said the Alchemist, insulted to his core.

The Boy picked up an iron cauldron and threw it across the room, knocking over a shelf and crashing through several of the tubes overhead. All colors of liquid dripped to the floor.

"Well, aren't you clever?" said the Alchemist. "Stolen one of my potions. You're a thief, but at least you're not as dumb as a cow or a lamb. Not that it will save you."

He ran up to his table of potions, grinned at the Boy, grabbed up a large cask of strength potion and downed it all in one gulp.

He paused, with a strange look on his face, cleared his throat, smacked his lips, fell over and died.

The Boy retrieved the orange.

"But what happened?" said the Girl.

"I switched the strength potion. Before I found you."

"Amazing! You switched it with the sleeping potion?"

"No. The death potion."

They walked past the table of potions. The Girl saw the sleeping potion, undisturbed, sitting next to where the death potion had been when the Alchemist picked it up.

They fled the Alchemist's castle. Outside, they rushed back down the path, back through the shrine and kept going until they found a stream. They jumped in, clothes and all. It was cold, but they stayed in it a long time, scrubbing at their skin and clothes. After getting as clean as they could they got out and shivered in the air.

"We need to find new clothes," said the Boy.

They were glad to be back on the road, with the mountain far behind them. They didn't speak of the Alchemist and his laboratory. The first night the Girl began to shake and the Boy came over and held her, though his arms were hardly more steady. The days were better, filled as they were with walking.

They saw no one until the afternoon that two men, a tall one and a short one, appeared in the distance, coming towards them. Once they were close enough to see into the men's faces the Boy was uneasy. The two servants never took their eyes off him. When they came to the same place the two servants stood with their feet wide, blocking the way.

"Do you have anything to share with two poor travelers far from home?"

"No," said the Boy.

"No, you're not going to share anything, are you?"

"What?"

"You heard him."

"And what about this pretty girl? If love is your main course, is she your dessert?"

The Boy stood in front of the Girl. "I have no quarrel."

"As long as you have what you like and others are left wanting you have no quarrel."

"Does that seem fair to you?"

"Be on your way," said the Boy.

"You be on your way!"

The servants pulled out their knives and stabbed him. The Girl screamed. The Boy looked down at his wounds as though he wasn't sure how they got there. The two servants looked down at their blades, and their hands covered with blood, and ran off like rabbits.

The Boy collapsed to one knee, then both, and the Girl helped him down onto his back. She pressed her hands against his wounds. Sobs came out from deep within her.

192

Looking around, she began shouting for help. She heard a voice behind her.

"Am I too late? What's happened here?" said Sileno.

"Please help!"

Sileno knelt over the Boy, gently easing the Girl aside. "What's happened?"

"I don't know. Two men. I don't know." She broke down in tears. "Please. He can't leave me."

"He's badly hurt."

"Will he be all right?"

"He needs water. Fetch some from the stream. Now. Go!"

She ran to the stream as fast as she could. Sileno took a cloth out of his pocket and wiped away blood, then pressed it against his wounds.

"It's not too late for you. Your love for the Princessa has brought all this trouble on you. I can take away that love. I can take it away and heal your wounds."

"What are you talking about?"

"Forget the Princessa. You will live. Take this pretty flower girl home with you and start a life together. She is a fine girl. It would be a fine life."

"I can't."

"I think you should."

"And if I refuse?"

"You will die and there's nothing I can do. I am sorry."

Sileno sat for a time next to the Boy as he lay on the ground, each breath a struggle.

"Do you have an answer?" said Sileno.

"Anyone can be in love when it's easy and feels good. My heart would sooner change place with another organ than change who it's for."

"I see."

"What now?" he said with shallow breath.

"Complete your task, if you wish."

"The oranges? But..." The Boy turned on his side and

rummaged through his bag. He pulled out the three oranges.

"I love these oranges. Each one of them. Because I must. Because they remind me of her. Because if I can love an orange so well, imagine how I will be able to love her."

The Boy took out a knife and cut open an orange. He put the halves one by one to his mouth and devoured and swallowed the pulp and juice until nothing but some of the peel was left. Then he did the same thing with the next orange. And again with the last one.

"How is it?" said Sileno.

"Wonderful." And the Boy died.

The Girl returned from the stream with water cupped in her hands. She knelt next to him, ready to dribble cool water onto his lips, but she saw his eyes closed, and his breath still, and she realized he was gone. Lost to her. The water trickled through her fingers.

"No…" she whispered. She quietly wept. Tears dampened the Boy's cold cheeks. She sat up and stared down at him.

"Will I always think of him like this, or will I think of how he was?" she said.

"I have no experience in these things."

Nothing was said for some time. At last Sileno spoke.

"Help me bury him. He's gone forever, I can do nothing about that, but I promise you, next year an orange tree will grow in this spot. The finest and tallest orange tree any of us have seen."

He stopped at her peculiar expression. "What?"

"I'm just wondering what will grow in the Ogre's garden."

They buried the Boy. It was hard work, and when they were done they washed up at the stream and returned to the grave. There was no eulogy. The Girl simply said he would be missed, and let her tears fall on the ground. She gathered a batch of flowers for his grave then, there being nothing left to be done about it, they turned away.

"The worst hurts change what we are. But you don't have

to change. You can go back to how you were," said Sileno.

"What?"

"I can make it so you don't love him. So you don't hurt."

"Like a potion."

"Not like that."

"Would I forget?"

"No. You'd remember. But you wouldn't feel it."

"You can do such a thing?"

"I can."

"Why would you do that?"

"You're a strong and brave girl. I'd like to help you."

"When I was little I heard a story about a girl who loved someone like she loved salt. It made food taste better, but sometimes it hurt. My love is like salt."

"I can wash the salt from your wound."

"No. I'll keep what's mine. Thank you."

The Girl put her sack over her shoulder and began her long journey home.

The Princessa awoke. It was a bright, clear morning. She went out into the hall, then walked downstairs. All her guards were asleep. She idly wandered the kitchen and dining hall, sweeping everything with her gaze, and stepped out the front door, which was partly open.

Sileno was there, to one side.

"It is done," he said.

She smiled. Gave him a small hug. Then she walked down to the beach, Sileno close behind. She took off her shoes, bent down, and put them on dry sand where she knew the waves couldn't reach, and walked barefoot into the surf. She sucked in her breath at the coldness of the water. Thrilled with the unexpectedness of it.

Just beneath the sound of the waves she heard a beautiful,

unearthly song. She hesitated. Turned to Sileno.

"Now you are free, my Princessa."

She waded into the water, and kept walking out into the ocean until the tide swept her away never to return.

The Princessa's shoes were brought to the King. He said nothing, but retired to his quarters. From then the King kept to his dark room, bed-ridden with grief. He had servants around him, and sometimes friends, all ready to fulfill his wishes. But he asked for nothing.

Except for one time, when he asked for his advisor, Sileno. Word went through the palace, and soon Sileno sat alone with the King.

"Sire. You suffer much. Love ravages your body. I can make it so you let it go."

"You can remove the pain?"

"I can remove the love. The pain comes with it."

"Truly?"

"Yes."

"What are you?"

"Just a loyal servant."

"But who's?"

A shrug. A sympathetic smile. "They are gone. They can't come back. This serves nothing. Give me your hand."

"Away from me." The King turned his head to the wall.

"Of them all, of the many, you I understand the least. But say the word and you will be whole. You will rise from this bed. You will rule again. You will even laugh."

"It is a sin to make it as though they were never here at all."

He would say nothing else.

So Sileno walked out the palace gate and was never seen again. The King had his two servants killed for their failure to save the Princessa. They were not remarkable for kindness or goodness, but they were loved and their families wept bitterly. The unimportant people of the kingdom would sometimes look up at the palace as they passed by, and say he was once a good and powerful King. The King lived to a ripe old age, though if he ever stepped out of his quarters again it is not remembered. What is remembered is what his bedside servants said of his fitful, mumbling sleep. He sometimes dreamed of an orange, full and round, unblemished dimpled rind, juicy, tender, sweet, a perfect orange.

END

About the Author

As a child Jeff Solmundson was led astray by comic books into all sorts of other strange and wayward tales in various mediums, leading to an incurable fascination with narrative. In his spare time he likes to pull stories apart and put them back together again.

Solmundson has at times been a public relations rep, newspaper editor, magazine writer, tree planter, college radio station deejay and an amateur detective feigning blindness. *Long ago, far away* is his first story collection.

He lives in Winnipeg, Manitoba, Canada. All in all, not a bad place to live and work. Summer is wonderful. As for its counterpart, the 19th century settlers who perished leaving behind nothing but shallow graves and their diaries, said it best: "Winters are hard."